THE PONY EXPRESS RIDER

Ron Bell

Ronnie Campbell Series Book 1

This is a work of fiction with historical facts mixed in to make a good story. Many of the names are of persons I have known over the years and have been placed back into the 1860 time period. None of these people lived in this time but, if they did, they may have found themselves riding for the Pony Express.

ISBN: 0615799604

ACKNOWLEDGMENTS

I would like to thank some of the people who helped me get this book ready to publish. First to Sandy Blair who talked me into adding to the short story reflected in the prolog. Mandy Bennett also was a great help by helping with the editing process. My wife Susan Bell who finished going through the book and helping me make the changes needed to bring the book to the finish.

The photo work in the book was supplied by Richard Massey along with Sarah Morey and Nick McCabe. Thanks also to Fort Churchill State Park for allowing these photos to be taken.

Foreword

The Prologue is kind of a joke on me. With that being said, what happened during that time has changed my life in many ways. The Pony Express was a thing I drove by on my way to Carson City and said, :Has look at the horses" and stopped along Highway 50 to talk to one of the riders.

I now ride the re-ride each year. I now have four horses at my house and ride some each week. Some could be up to 25 to 50 miles each week depending on the weather and work schedule.

The Pony Express is part of my life, I hope you enjoy the adventures of the young man Ronnie Campbell, the second book is under way. You will find a preview in the back of this book. You have heard the words, Pay Back is Hell, or is it a Ride into Hell?

Ron Bell AKA Ronnie Campbell

Fort Churchill State Park, Picture by Nick McCabe

The Pony Express Rider
By Ron Bell

Silver Springs, Nevada

Prologue: The Ride That Changed My Life

My first Pony Express ride 2011

Sand Mountain to Top Gun

Larry McPherson, past president of the Pony Express and former Lyon County Commissioner, is a friend of mine. One of his biggest joys is seeing the Pony Express rider outline on top of the hill at Moundhouse, a small community located seven miles east of Carson City. This twelve-foot high steel cutout, a silhouette, commemorates famous riders who rode through this area of Nevada, and Larry went to great lengths to erect this memorial. It was there for a long time, until a very high wind blew it over, and that's when Larry began to receive calls asking what had happened to it. Did he have it removed?

Well, the story of how it was restored starts now.

Larry asked me, "Don't you weld?"

"Most of my life," I said, "Why?"

A high wind knocked the silhouette rider down and he needed help to put it back up, by welding the angle iron supports to the cement base. . . "This will restore it to its former position," Larry replied. And then he informed me, "I contacted a fellow rider and contractor by the name of Arthur Johnson. He has a skid steer loader that can lift up the twelve hundred pound piece of steel and put it back into place." When the day came to re-install the Horse and Rider on the hill outside Moundhouse, a crew arrived with trucks and a front loader. We were set to go. That's when the wind started to blow - when Arthur and his helper started cutting steel and I began to weld. Two hours later mission was accomplished, and since it was done in a good stiff wind, our work was load tested.

As we worked putting up the silhouette, Larry told me about a Pony Express re-ride that takes place every year. Two days later, he asked me if I wanted to join a team that was being assembled to make the Pony Express re-ride from Sand Mountain to Top Gun, which is just outside Fallon, Nevada.

My answer – perhaps a bit too quick, was, "That would be fun. Count me in with both feet."

*

Now, let's get the stage set – I had no hat, no western shirt – and another minor thing – I had no horse or saddle, and yet I had opened my mouth. Did I mention that I had ridden a horse only a few times in the past few years? I didn't worry about it because I was told that when you climb up on a horse again it will come back to you like when you used to team rope and ride all the time. Yes, I used to do that, but I'm not going to tell you how many years ago it was.

Did I mention not having a horse? Well, I asked a friend if I could use one of hers and when she said yes, I thought I was home free. But now I did not have a saddle, and that's when up pops Larry, who said, "Just use my extra saddle."

Okay, I'm moving right along now, when another change, in getting ready for the ride, came up a couple of days later. I was getting some miles on this horse, but the owner of the horse started having problems– one concern was the possibility that we might ride at night and the other was the fact that I was also a little plump in some places. And when you add the 40 pound mailbag to all this, it was decided my plan might not work. That's when I told Larry, "Hey Larry, I'm going to drop out, because of the horse problem."

"Whooooa!" he said, which is a horse term meaning STOP! "Give me a couple of days to ask around. Maybe we need two horses." And a couple days later, he called to say he had found them.

Well – off I go to test one of the two. We went out and had a great ride, but I felt this guy (meaning the horse) did not have a good throttle. I was going to ride over a rough section of trail that was broken up with an outcropping of rocks. The area I had to go over had short distances that would require I walk and pick the path on foot. On other portions I could rev up a little and in other places I could click up and go full out. So off I go to check out the second horse.

Here I am, getting down to a week and a few days left, trying to know a new horse and to get us both in shape for the ride - when along comes Dandy. Dandy is a killer looking horse - a classic quarter horse, in other words, a great looking animal. The owner, Gary Rogers, and I decided that I should take Dandy home with me so I could ride him every day. Well, that was great but, first, I needed to fix him a place that he could call his own.

Two days later, after having installed new wooden posts for one gate, I added horse wire, repaired a couple more gates and in general, managed to rebuild a more substantial corral than I had already in the back yard. And finally, I was ready to ride Dandy from his owner's house to mine for a short visit.

Did I mention that Dandy had only been ridden a few times in the last few years and that he had some great friends he had lived with for years? He did not like going anywhere without them. After a few false starts, and after telling him that he'd be okay in his new home, we moved along, in a zigzag pattern, until I got him to his new home.

Over the next few days we came to an agreement. I was going to be the boss and he was going to move my fat (or rather plump) body along at a good clip. he also wanted to check out other places along the way, trying to find his friends to tell them that he was having problems with the guy who was feeding him.

Dandy can move, but anything other than a walk was a killer for me. I do think that his shocks needed to be replaced, and I was told that I would have to take some punishment myself to attain the glory I was seeking. On one of my daily five-mile rides, I found out how fast he really could move – I would say, really fast – from one side of the road to the other. He could make this move in about three jumps but I stayed with him. This is when I knew I was getting back some of the abilities I used to have.

The problem was this - can you believe it - Dandy freaked out over horse cutouts that were on a fence we rode by. It was some kind of yard art. We talked it over and I led him to see the big mean cutouts, one step at a time, and when the issue was resolved, we were back on the road.

When Ride Day came, I asked Dandy if he wanted to go for a little trip. I guess he did because he jumped into Larry's trailer and promptly took a dump. I think he felt right at home. Since Larry was the one who started this little adventure, it was only right that he got to clean out the trailer. Surely the swept up stuff would help his flowers grow.

We got to the staging area at the beginning of our thirty-mile trail. Here, the ride captain and riders meet and relax as we wait for the other riders who are bringing the mail to us. When we know that the mail is getting close, we pull the horse trailers to the starting point and get the horses ready to go. As I waited, I took pictures and talked to the other riders, who were also waiting. Looking the part and having a horse that could do his part, the only thing left for me to do was to actually perform my part. I was ready.

Time was getting late when the mail got to our staging area. That's when things got going. I was up second, so Dandy was loaded and we were ready to move to my starting location. That's when Larry was asked if he would allow the Pony Express National President, Jim Swigart, to ride the first two miles.

When Larry said yes, it was decided that he would do the next leg of three miles and the change was made. The mailbag/mochila was thrown on the horse, the rider mounted. The horse, with its tail straight behind, head forward, and hooves beating fast, gave proof that the mail was continuing on its way.

We jumped into the truck and got ahead of the first rider in order to get Larry ready at the two-mile mark.. He had three miles to ride - to the water tanks, along the power line. When the first horse arrived, Larry was on his horse and in a cloud of dust he went off, down the trail.

It was hard work getting ahead of Larry, but we did. Down the road we went, to get to my starting point at the five-mile mark.. Here, I got Dandy out of the trailer, walked him around a little, pulled a little slack out of the cinch - and I was ready to ride.

Looking up the road, I could see that Larry was coming in fast. The sun was sinking fast as we made the mochila exchange onto my horse Dandy. I would like to say I jumped into the saddle, but I kind of got my foot in the stirrup and hauled myself aboard. I asked Dandy if he would like to move along the road (well – kind of a road). After a short talk, we moved forward. I knew we had to move along better than a walk, so after a little more talking, and a little boot to his ribs, Dandy shook his head and we started to make our own dust.

I was concerned about the throttle and how we would walk over the bad stuff along the way. I was only able to get shoes on Dandy's front feet before the re-ride. And now, I did manage to move him around with the reins and a little leg, as I worked to find the best way to get over the rocks. Between the rock outcroppings we were able to get into second gear - then down to first again over the next bunch of rocks. This went on until I got to some soft-sand stretches where using a little boot heel, I clicked him up, and off we went at full throttle for a short time – and then back to first gear over more rocks.

I am now feeling like I belong on this ride with the mailbag, or mochila, under me. Dandy is running flat out, eating up the ground, heading for the exchange. As we galloped down the trail, my mind began to wander back in time, remembering conversations with friends about the Pony Express. Setting around the campfire in the evening, we discussed those names of the great Pony Express riders. When our talk turned to stories about what those great riders did and the dangers they faced I need to do my part to show respect to the great riders.

Well - this is the tale of just one of the many who rode. His name never was in lights. In fact, little if anything was ever heard of him after the Pony Express quit delivering mail in 1861.

Ronnie Campbell is a person I would have liked to be if I had been alive in this time period. When I started to write this book I started to think how I would have lived in this time period along with what tools did I have to use going forward with my life. I feel the gold had to be the center of the story.

I am Ronnie Campbell, fourteen years old, living in New Haven, Connecticut with my parents Dick and Louise (Jim, her nickname) Campbell. This is my story as I remember it.

Chapter 1 LOOSING PA

Year 1859 - (Ruby Mountains?) Nevada

When the hills were just starting to show light, Pa shook me out of bed and said, "Get your rifle and start tracking the team."

Winter had been on and off for most of the past few months. There still was some snow in the shady spots, but it never stayed too long. The cold weather had been keeping us from panning for gold in the stream for over a month now. Some dry grass remained along the stream's bank although the horses had cleaned off most of it close to the house. I had to picket the horses upstream during the day, and bring them into the corrals at night. In the last few weeks we did have a little rain and new grass was just coming on now.

That morning Pa told me, "Bill got the top rail down again, and Sally went with him. You may have a long walk to find 'em." Getting into my pants, boots and pulling a shirt over my head, I grabbed my jacket off the peg by the door. I was about to go out into the cold morning when Pa said, "Grab a couple of biscuits and cut yourself a slab of meat. It's time to get started. You're burning daylight. There's no telling when they got out and how far away they may be by now."

February could bring most any type of weather. Give it a day or two and you can have about anything that might come along. Bill had a bad habit of grabbing the top rail, sliding it over, then walking out of the corral. I should have tied the rail off with rope but I had forgotten.

We had not used Bill and Sally for a few days, so I found their tracks right off, heading toward the hills to the north. There wasn't much of a chance of missing their tracks since they both had big feet and each weighed around 2000 pounds. They were long of leg, and they were stepping out like they had some place to go.

I walked for most of the morning, working their trail. It looked like they were heading for the little valley that was about five miles from our house. It had a small stream running down the center with willows growing along its banks. The hills on each side of the valley had pine trees growing up to the top of the ridge. Its a real nice spot. "I might want to have a cabin in this valley sometime.

Just a few months ago, Pa spent a couple of days there pulling some logs out for firewood. Thinking that maybe the horses liked the grass along the stream and would head there, I decided to take a shortcut and see if they had made it that far. I came to a game trail that angled up the side of the hill, among the pines, heading for a saddle between two low hills. Behind the hills lay the valley.

The climb was slow, but if I was right, I could save a couple of the hours it would have taken for me to skirt the line of hills and reach the mouth of the valley. I knew I was taking a chance on finding them there. If I was wrong, I would have to go back and pick up their old tracks. When I got to the top of the saddle, I was breathing hard. I stopped to take a look around and catch my breath. Not seeing the horses, I dropped down the back side, to the creek below, to get a drink and wash my face.

Just as I got to the creek I saw the tracks. They looked fresh. My short cut had paid off. Feeling like I was close, I felt they would stay to the lower ground along the water, because the grass was better there. Working my way up the valley I found Bill. He was just grazing along the stream, and he let me walk right up to him, where I put the halter and lead rope on him. With Bill on the lead rope, I was able to get Sally after a couple of tries, even if she wasn't ready to be caught. With the two horses ready to go I decided to sit on a rock and eat my biscuit and meat that was in my pocket before heading home. After getting a drink, I started leading Bill and Salley back down along the small stream, looking for a high spot so I could mount Bill. That's when I saw smoke coming from the direction of our cabin.

*

Bill was a big brown gelding; too tall for me to mount without having something to stand on. I was all of fourteen years old; a touch small for my age. I found a rock along the trickle of water coming down from the hills, emptying into the larger stream. I got Bill into the water below the rock so I could get aboard.

That's when I happened to look down, and something caught my eye. It was a small gold nugget sitting in the black sand by the rock. I got off the rock and picked it up from the cold water. The nugget was not a large one, but it was bigger than what we had been getting out of the main stream we had been working. After wiping my hands on my pants, I stuck the nugget into my pocket, got on Bill's back, and headed for home. Pa would be interested in hearing where I found it.

With a halter and lead rope on Sally, off we went back down the stream leading to the short cut. A small game trail rising up to the saddle between the hills I walked over earlier. When I got to the top, I stopped to look over the valley toward home. It was then I saw that our cabin was burning, and I heard the gunfire. Pa was alone, and I could hear the Henry rifle talking.

"Pa bought his new repeating rifle from the factory before we headed west. Mr. Tayler Henry sold it to him in person. Tayler knew that Pa was going west, and he told Pa it was one of the first test rifles of a new type he had just invented. And sure enough, it would come in handy on our trip west. It held 15 bullets and, right now, I could hear that he was using them fast."

I made the best time I could on Bill, who was better at pulling the wagon than making speed along a trail. And then I heard the loudest sound you will ever hear in your life, total silence. The Henry was not talking any more, and I was still better than two miles from home.

Working my way to the edge of the trees, I stopped. I was still about two hundred yards out; a long rifle shot to the house. Here I saw the cabin was just about burned to the ground and part of the barn was still on fire. Pa was lying on the ground just outside of the cabin door. At this point, there wasn't much I could do, so I waited, checking to see if the Indians had a mind to come back.

After waiting a while, I went in to see if I could do anything for Pa. He was dead, hit with two arrows and one bullet. I broke off the arrows and moved Pa back under the tree by Ma's grave. Then I checked to see what was left. Taking note of the damage, I saw that all of the stock was gone. The Henry rifle and Pa's Navy Colt pistol were gone also. I checked the tracks and it looked like the Indian who picked up Pa's Henry was riding a horse that toed in a bit on its right front hoof. It also looked like Pa had killed five Indians.

He must have been caught in the open, unable to make it to safety, inside the cabin. I could see that he made his final stand in the front yard. I could not remember how many times I heard his rifle shoot that day.

It looked like Pa killed the five Indians at close range because there were signs of five dead bodies only yards from him in front of the cabin. And there were no signs of movement after they hit the ground, just some blood. All that was left from the fight was five separate pools of blood on the ground. The Indians had taken their dead and wounded away.

Looking around, I did find three more drag marks and a lot more blood a little further out from the cabin. From what I could tell, that bunch paid a high price for the raid, but I was the one who paid the higher price - my Pa. It looked like they must have respected his courage and ability to fight, because he was not cut up or scalped. At least this was a little bit for me to hold onto.

I spent the rest of the day digging Pa's grave next to Ma's, so they could be together at last. I remember how they used to sit outside and whisper to each other for hours; maybe they can still talk. Ma had passed some time ago, and Pa was all I had to call family. I sat there beside their graves, thinking back to when we headed west. It seemed like a long time ago, but in reality, it was not that long. With my Ma and Pa gone, I wondered what I was going to do now. Alone in the back-country, I was a few days ride from any other people.

Chapter 2 HEADING WEST

Looking back at it, it seems like a long time ago. The day I was told we were coming west, I was out hunting deer. When I got to the house with a nice buck, Pa said, "We're heading west in a few weeks. Going to Nevada."

When I asked him why, he said, "I talked to a man named Gary Rogers, who said he found some gold nuggets in Eastern Nevada. He said he found them in a creek that's two or three days ride north of a small store. The owner of the store is a man called Jim Brown. We're going to go and find that place."

"Who is Gary Rogers?" I said.

"He was a wagon train guide."

"So he must know the area."

"I guess. He traveled over many of the early trails leading out of St. Louis. That is, until he received a letter telling him his brother died and left him a shipping business in New Haven, Connecticut. At the time he was in California, where he met some people who wanted to return east. They needed a guide, and he agreed to take them as far as St. Louis."

As I learned from Pa, as this man Gary led them east, a couple wagons had some problems. Therefore the little wagon train stopped at Mr. Browns store, south of the Ruby Mountains in Nevada. Since he had a week or so to kill while the wagons were being repaired, Gary took a ride north into the hills just to look around.

As Pa put it, "The land was a pretty sight. Each cut in the mountain had water flowing into the valley below. Willows grew along the bank, with grass covering the flats between the hillsides. On his third day out Gary came to a flat spot with trees for protection from the wind. He decided this is a good place to camp. Gary decided to set up camp early for the night. He walked along the stream looking for signs of fish. He carried string and hooks in his saddle bags, just in case he might come across a good fishing hole."

"He didn't worry about Indians or any kind of danger, out there alone?" I asked.

"Well . . . since he was deep into the backcountry, there were considerations he had to make . . . like deciding not to fire his rifle to kill any game unless he absolutely needed to. No telling who might hear it and come to pay a visit. Gary knew he was in the Pah Ute's hunting grounds. According to Gary, this is a tribe who doesn't cause anyone much trouble. Well, it was known they would steal a horse or two if they had a chance, but Gary kept his horse in close to his camp at all times. And he had his rifle ready to use in case he needed it.

Pa gave me Gary's story like this - Walking a short distance, alongside the creek, Gary spotted a pebble that looked like gold. He picked it up and to his amazement discovered it was a good sized nugget. Forgetting the fish, he moved further up the bank and found a few more. He put them in his pocket before we went back to his camp to fix dinner. He planned on starting his two day return trip back to the store. He reached the store late on the second day to lead his wagon train east to St Louis.

"How did you learn about it, Pa?" I asked.

"He is a close friend of Mr. Benjamin Henry the rifle maker, and we have talked many times over the past year."

"Gary said he never told anybody but me. He thought he was going to go back, but when he knew he wasn't, that's when he told me."

The area Gary was talking about is located in the Ruby Mountains in Nevada, just west of the Utah border. Dick (my Pa) and Louise (Jim) Campbell (my Ma) talked it over before deciding to make the trip. Ma's health had been going downhill for the last year and she felt the change of climate would do her good. When I was told about it, all I could think about was seeing Indians and tall mountains, never having an idea of just how long this trip would be.

From what Pa had heard, the Indians had not been any kind of problem over the last few years. "But remember this!" he told me. "Indians can change their minds in a flash. Until you establish some kind of relationship with them, you do need to be on guard. It is well known that when they go on a raid, it may have been caused by some other event, in another area . . . and if it was, you may not have been involved in the problem or even know about what caused it or what happened."

And then he warned me. "When you are out in the wild, keep your weapons loaded and close at hand. Keep watch for tracks back in the hills and around your home. I have heard the natives might watch what you do each day for a while.

"Are they dangerous?"

"I don't think so, but to be on the safe side, don't do the same thing every day. You might need to make a trade with the Indians for land. Remember this . . . it is their land, and until you make some kind of deal with them, they may not like you building a cabin."

For a young boy, this was going to be exciting, for sure.

*

Ma and Pa were getting things together when our neighbor, Mr. Taylor Henry came over to talk to Pa. Since he was a gunsmith, he asked if Pa would like to take one of his new test rifles; telling him it would be mighty handy in an Indian fight. "It shoots like new," he said. "In fact, I have sold some to the Union Army! And they will start taking delivery in about six to eight months from now." As my Pa learned, this new rifle was not like any other. It could shoot fifteen rounds without reloading. His old rifle was a Spencer, and it only held six rounds.

It took a couple of weeks for Pa to get a wagon and purchase the four horses we would need to pull our wagon load of our possessions. Pa and Mr. Rogers picked out the equipment we would need to make the trip and set up our home. Having the wagon loaded with supplies and Ma's things, we headed west.

For a boy of thirteen, I was just starting on a big adventure. It took a couple weeks of traveling before we crossed the Ohio River and headed west. Ma was having problems with the cold damp days and nights, and I heard her having trouble breathing during the night. I slept under the wagon seat if the weather was real bad. But most times, I just made a bed under the wagon, sleeping with a canvas tarp, folded under and over me to keep out the weather.

I heard them talking about Nevada having a drier climate, and Ma said, "Doctor Smith says it will do me good." She was not having an easy time of it, that's for sure.

I drove the four-horse team, so Pa could tend to Ma in their bed in the back of the wagon. Pa had purchased four of the best horses he could find. Bill and Sally were the wheel team horses, and Maud and Florey were the two lead team horses.

We could have gotten by with only two horses, but Pa said, "One might get sick and die along the way." Pa was like that, always thinking ahead, trying to avoid any problem that might catch up to you, unexpected like.

Many a night I was glad for the bed in the front of the wagon. We had rain, hail, and snow most of the way, and at times the mud was bad on the wagon roads we took heading west. We were glad that we had four horses to pull the wagon. Pa and I both worked through a few sets of gloves and that was before we were halfway to St. Louis.

As it was slow going, we needed the weather to clear some, and we also hoped for an early spring. But things got worse as we traveled down the road. On this one particular day, light snow started about noon. We had just rested the horses and put them on grass and water while we ate a bit of lunch. After we got started again, the snow started to fall with larger flakes, and, as they were heavy with water, the snow built up on the road fast. Drifts were forming.

I turned to Pa and asked, "Should we find a sheltered spot with some water and grass?"

"Okay," he said. "If you see a spot, pull in and we'll unhook".

I drove on, heading west, for another hour until I saw a small stream crossing the road ahead of us. Luck would have it there was a nice clearing and I was able to pull the team and wagon under a large oak tree. It would help keep the snow off the wagon top. Pa did not come out of the back of the wagon after I had made the stop. After unhitching the horses and having them on picket line close to the water, I went back to see if he and Ma were okay.

Ma was asleep. He said, "Get Bill and ride up the trail a few miles. See if you can find a town or ask someone if there's a doctor somewhere close. Your mom is not doing very well."

While he started a fire to warm some water for Mom, I went and got Bill from the picket line. Using the wagon tongue to get on his back, Bill and I started down the road. I rode until dark then turned back to our camp without finding any help. The snow was still falling and getting deeper. I was covered with snow and Bill looked like a white horse even though, underneath it all, he was brown.

After the sun went down it was getting colder. I hoped that Pa had a fire going. When I got back to the wagon, I saw two other wagons pulled in beside ours, and I did see a good fire blazing away. Coming to the other horses, I slid off Bill and tied him back on the picket line.

Pa called me over to the fire, to meet our new friends. They had two kids my age - Les Warren and Hartley Close. When I looked in the back of the wagon, Ma was sitting up looking out. One of the new ladies was sitting on the back of the wagon with her, and they were talking. It was the first time in a week that I had seen Ma sitting up. Pa said, "Your mother's fever dropped just after you rode off." I found out the other wagons were heading for California to work in the gold fields.

Pa told our new friends we were going to raise some cattle and horses in Nevada. To me, in private, he said, "Don't talk about trying to find gold to anyone at any time."

The next morning we all headed west to St. Louis, hoping to find more wagons to join up with, going to Nevada. Driving out of the clearing, the wagons were almost silent, due to the deep snow. The only sound was the jingle of the trace chains as we moved along. Pa was the only one who had extra horses for the trip. As he said, "It will save our horses, because they have less weight to pull."

After a mile or so, and because our team was able to move faster than the others, Pa had me pull over and wait for them. We waved them by and pulled in behind the last wagon. It took a couple of hours for our horses to get used to the slower pace, but we stayed behind everyone else for the rest of the trip to St. Louis. Things went well during the balance of the trip to St. Louis. We arrived a week before the next wagon train was scheduled to depart for the west.

When it was time to leave St. Louis, we paid the wagon master, and picked up last minute supplies. Now we were ready to finally head west to Nevada. To my relief, Ma was sitting on the wagon seat when we got underway. She had recovered some of her strength and was feeling much better. I think it helped for her to have other ladies around. Pa and I could now handle the stock and not have to worry about her. Over the next few months we took turns driving and walking beside the wagon to save weight for the horses. From what the guide told us we were making good time up to this point in our trip. We had missed Indian trouble so far and were hopeful to keep it that way. We were working our way on to Salt Lake City making about 25 miles per day. At Salt Lake City we re-supplied and headed for Jim Brown's store.

The first day out of Salt Lake City, the team of one of our friends quit pulling. They just laid down. It was at the south end of the Great Salt Lake, and it had been hard pulling. The wagons were half way up to the hubs in sand. Twice that day, Pa had me hook a chain to their wagon to pull them out of deep sand pockets.

After doing it a couple times, the wagon-master came back and told us we could not stop for longer than a few hours. We had to move on, one way or another, which meant we had to get the horses up and ready to go or we would have to leave them behind. Pa unhooked our two lead horses. After moving them to the other wagon, we hooked our extra team to it and had the wagon pull in behind ours. We could not make the two tired horses get up. They had pulled their last. Stripping off the gear, Mr. Warren had no choice but to shoot them - and we all resumed driving west, heading for the Nevada border.

Later that day, Pa said, "Since we're close to where we're headed, I'm going to sell Maud and Florey to Mr. Warren. We only need Bill and Sally anyway, and the money will come in handy until we find some gold."

It took a few more days to reach the store - Jim Brown's store. After taking a small rest, Pa set about getting supplies to last us for six months or so.

When Mr. Brown asked Pa, "What are you going to do here?"

Pa said, "Well, I just want to find a nice place to settle down. I will see what I want to do later."

Mr. Brown said to Pa, "You best keep a close watch for Indians, we have not had any problems with them yet. Now you are going into the back country and you are the first that I know about in that area, so do keep a close watch. We want you to come back to town from time to time."

Ma came over to Mr. Brown and asked if he knew about any Indian raids in the area. He said that he had not heard of any trouble for a long while. Pa told Mr. Brown that he had one of the best rifles made and it could shoot 15 times. Jim told Pa that he had seen some information on this rifle in a newspaper a few months back.. Mr. Brown said that he would order some ammunition for our rifle.

With supplies loaded, Pa stepped up onto the wagon and slapped the reins on the horses' flanks and they moved out.

From Jim Brown's store, we headed northwest, working our way around the south end of the Ruby mountain range. Whenever we came to a creek, Pa and I tested it for gold. Finding none, we kept moving further north.

After days of panning, we pulled into a nice flat area about twenty acres in size, by a fast running stream. The ground sloped up as you got close to the rock face.. After close inspection, we discovered a small seep coming from the rock wall. Pa said, "Let's stay here for a few days. Ronnie, you and I will branch out to cover more of the stream. Ma started to set up camp hoping this would be our final move. That would depend on what we found in this stream. We hit some color right off. Pa got a pan with a couple of small nuggets - and, on the same day, I found some flake gold.

Feeling pretty good, we set about building our cabin, along with a small barn to store hay and a small tool shed on the backside. Pa put the team to work skidding logs down from the hills. I was in charge of trimming the limbs and peeling bark off the logs. He informed me, "If we don't peel the bark from the logs, we will have a mess when we start a fire. There are beetles and other bugs in the bark, just waiting to hatch. With a fire, they will think it is spring and they'll run us out of the cabin. We'll be eaten alive.

I also had the task of digging out the side of the hill to make a root cellar. After I got the cave or root cellar dug, Pa showed me how to make a cooler using grain sacks over a wooden frame. Then he let some water drop on the bags to keep them wet. He said, "The air will evaporate the water and the inside of the bags will be cool."

Hot damn! It worked! I dammed up an area to make a pool to collect water for the house. We also split logs to make boards to use as the door.

We needed to finish the cabin as fast as possible because winter was on its way. Pa and I set our axes to notching the logs so they would fit close together. Ma mixed clay and grass to make a seal between the logs to keep the wind out. She was keeping up with us. Ma was breathing better now and could work a little. We would set a log and she would seal it with clay and grass mixture, right behind us. When we got part of the roof on the walls, she moved the stove into her new cabin. Now she had a fireplace to work with, and also a stove. Ma was happy!

Talk about feeling good! Ma was going to fix a meal indoors for the first time in over a year. I had killed a deer that same morning, and she was going to fry up some steaks with wild onions we found and stored in the cold cellar. After our meal Pa and I continued to split logs to make the last few boards for the roof on the cabin.

Ma was feeling good. Her breathing had improved and her color was getting better. As she was big on book learning, she made me take time out from panning gold to study. Every week she kept pulling out another book for me to look at. I found out I was good at math. The English was tough, but Ma kept at me, insisting I was going to learn. After I tried to sneak off and hunt instead of doing my bookwork - she took some bark off me with a belt. After a few times, she put an end to that idea of taking off to go hunt.

During that very first winter, Ma suddenly got sick and died. It was just before Christmas - a hard time for Pa and me. Pa was good at telling me about things I would need to know, but he was not much on the books. With just the two of us, we could never find time for me to study. Work and hunting was at the top of the list of things I had to do.

Looking back at it, when Ma and Pa were together, all those talks now sat heavy on my shoulders. Our little spread was not much to look at - but we made it do. As we washed some gold from the stream, we also kept looking for the main vein. Up to now, we had only panned enough gold to keep us in the basics - like flour, salt, beans and such. It was a hard two-day ride from Mr. Brown's store. I still had the team, Bill and Sally, but the wagon had burned during the Indian raid. Therefore I had to ride Bill if I needed to go anyplace. Sally did not take to the riding part very well. I tried a few test rides on her, but found it was simpler to just ride Bill.

And now I had to take stock of my situation and think back on what Pa had been telling me. After Ma died he had taken the time, most every night, to talk about all of the things I would need to know if he ever was not around. Most of his basic instructions were to take your time and look at the long term - like one to two years ahead.

I remember him telling me that gold is a good thing, but it will change even your best friends when you have it and they don't. Never tell anyone that you have very much. Many people find a nugget from time to time, so play that card. What I mean by that, is never let anyone know you have more than a few nuggets, and never tell anybody about gold dust. It will only trigger problems. Having gold dust means you are working a claim, and you could have a lot more stashed some place. You can bet they will come looking!

When we find the real gold, he had said, our plan is to travel hundreds of miles to put it in a bank to get some paper money. If any local finds out that we have gold, they will dog us until they find what we have. And then you can be sure they will do their best to take it .

Pa's idea of learning was to talk about how to get around in the woods. He told me, "Watch your back trail. If you think you should set a while, to see who is coming up behind you, you need to take that extra time, just to be sure you are alone."

"When you want to make a trade for something, be sure you work it so the other guy brings the idea to you - and never take the first deal. Remember - if they feel it is their idea, that you are helping them, they get what they want and you get what you want."

*

(What do I have left)? That was the big question now. The Indians missed the root cellar that was dug into the bank behind the house, where we had set aside some food and ammunition. Therefore I had rounds for my Spencer carbine. As I had been bringing in the meat for a long time, I knew I could make do for a while with just a few shells.

It looked like the root cellar was going to be my new home. What was I to do? Should I keep working the gold claim or try to find a job in town? That awful day – when the fire burned out, I looked to see if anything was worth trying to save. It looked bad. I could use some of the cooking pans, although they would take a lot of cleaning. I also found some of the tools in the shed on the backside of the barn that had not burned

After gathering up the burned dishes and cooking pans, I went to the creek and started washing them, using sand to get the smoke and ash off. I needed to build a lean-to that would cover the opening of the root cellar, and then I also needed to dig it a little bigger so I could put a bed on the back wall.

The next few days were spent getting a place to sleep and a covered place to cook. I decided I could build a small fire just inside the root cellar and let the smoke drift out over the top of the door. I had plenty of wood because of what Pa had pulled in – and what I had split before winter came. Now I needed to get some fresh meat. I cut new poles to rebuild the corral, so I could keep the two horses close to the dugout.

The next morning, I put a bridle on Bill and set off to go kill a deer or an elk. Riding back into the hills, past the gold claim, I started hunting. With Bill on a picket line, I set off on foot, working my way back further into the timbered hill country. Pa had me hunt in different directions from the cabin so as not to spook the game out of the area. This was the first time I had hunted this way in over six months or so. Working my way along the bottom of the draw, I found the trail that the game used to get down to the stream to drink. It was early in the afternoon, so I decided I would just wait.

Checking the wind and being well off the trail, I was ready. There was a small shift of wind. Now it was coming down off the mountain into my face. Anything coming to water could not smell me. With just a few shells, I needed to make the kill with one shot. The sun was getting lower and casting shadows when I heard the crunch of a leaf. I was ready with the Spencer laying across the top of a log aiming down the trail.

I knew I had to shoot low, like Pa had told me to do when shooting downhill. The deer stopped and stamped a foot, then stopped to look around. Slowly it took one step, then another. The deer was looking right and left, ears searching. Pa had said. "Now son, just put pressure back on the trigger but do not pull it, you should not know when it will fire." I sighted just behind the point of the buck's knee, easing pressure back on the trigger. The Spencer spoke and the deer was down. Now I had to get it dressed out and then go get Bill.

I can tell you, Bill did not like the smell of blood. In fact, he never liked it. But after wiping my bloody hands on his nose, he finally stood still so I could load the deer. With the deer loaded on Bill's back, I found a high spot so I could get on and hold the deer from falling off during the ride back to the dugout.

After hanging the deer on the crossbeam of the lean-to, I started cutting off the back strap to cook it like my Ma used to. She would then pound flour into the meat and would cook it in bacon grease. I got the fire started in the blackened stove. Dinner would be great tonight.

I had to smoke most of the meat and make jerky to preserve it. I found some wire that Pa had in the tool shed and made a wire rack. Then, I set up some wood poles beside a large rock face by the lean to. After building a small fire with some dry wood, I just kept adding green wood to the fire to smoke the meat.

As smoke rose up the rock wall - with the wire in place - I started adding meat to the wire rack. It was getting dark, so I had to build two other fires to be able to see enough to cut the meat into thin strips to smoke. The smoke was not doing a good job. The fire was heating the meat. What I needed was a way to hold in the smoke, so I set to building a box around the fire to direct the smoke over the meat along with the heat.

It was working just fine, but there was one more thing I had to do. I found a piece of wood to cover the top or at least most of the top. It kept most of the smoke inside of the box and around the meat. Working well into the night, I kept watch on the fire and added meat to the rack when needed. The jerky was looking good. By morning I had a bag of meat that would last for a while. After all that, I found a spot to keep watch and get some sleep.

Resting most of the day, I got to wondering how long I could live alone like this. Not knowing what to do, and having no one to ask, I decided I would just work the new creek for some gold and hope the Indians didn't come back. Being alone and all, Indians were strong on my mind. And at the same time, I was having a hard time dealing with the loss of both my Ma and Pa.

Mustangs by Richard Massey, photo taken close to Silver Springs Nevada.

Chapter 3 GETTING PA'S HENRY BACK

After a couple weeks, my meager supplies were about gone I had spent most of my time making repairs to what was left. I felt it was time to go back to the little valley where I had found the horses the day of the Indian raid.

This new stream looked better than what we had been working. I needed to spend a few days and do some panning to see just how good it was. The nuggets were a great find. They would come in handy down the road. At the same time, I also panned out a lot of loose gold which I put into a bag. When I started to feel the need to talk to someone, Bill turned an ear, but he never had a thing to say.

My first task was to make a plan to help me survive and keep my horses alive. I made a list of the things I needed to purchase in town such as some new pants because mine were getting thin and a mite too small and a hand scythe to cut hay in some of the upper meadows, to feed the horses during the coming winter. I also needed rope and blankets and some food stuffs. When I thought it out, I also realized I had to trade or sell both horses in order to get a better horse to ride and a packhorse. I set about gathering supplies that would last me for the two day ride into town.

First light found me working my way out of the hills, keeping close to the trees, so I could be on the watch for Indians. During the past few weeks, I had seen a set of tracks indicating an Indian pony whose front hoof toed in a little. I never saw the Indian or horse. I felt sure they belonged to the Indian that killed Pa, so I was watchful of my back trail on my ride to town.

At a small stream crossing, I spotted fresh hoof prints, just filling with water. It looked like they were put there less than an hour ahead of me - too close to suit me. The tracks led in the same direction I was going, so I eased back into the timber and waited for about an hour until the hair started to settle down on the back of my neck.

As it looked now, the two-day ride to town would be more like three if I planned to stay alive. With less than one box of shells, a gunfight would not be in my best interests. It made me wish that I had that new Henry and Navy Colt that were taken from my Pa. For now, the creek would have to give up more gold if I were to replace the Henry and Pa's pistol. Right now, all I had were my two horses, Bill and Sally, and my old Spencer rifle.

Keeping off the ridge tops and in the trees was costing me time, but I was taking it slow. Staying alive was the most important thing. When the sun was still high, I started looking for a sheltered spot so the horses could get on some grass and I could eat a little deer jerky. Seeing a trail leading toward the hills on my right and a small stream, I decided to give it a try.

After a bit, the trees opened into a small meadow. I had made a good choice. Picketing the horses near the stream so they could eat and drink, I then worked my way back down the trail for about a mile where I found a spot I could defend if need be. It had a good view of my back trail. I settled in behind a timber deadfall, two trees had fallen with a gap between them. I set about to eat some jerky and have a look see. Pa was a believer in moving slow and watching a lot. That's when I caught a flash of sun on metal. I had just about gotten up and headed back to the horses. Now I knew I had someone on my trail and I had to decide what I would do about it. If I was going to make it to town, I had to put a stop to whoever was dogging me. I was in a good spot. If there was someone tracking me, I needed to see him before he could see my tracks leading to the meadow.

Then I caught a slight bit of movement back in the trees. Someone was working my way. He was coming slowly, watching for any sign of movement. Time seemed to stand still. He was still coming on slow.

He must have figured that maybe I had gotten off the trail and was trying to cover my tracks. As I watched him, I realized that I was looking at Pa's Henry lying over his legs. He stopped and looked down, looking for my trail. I had never killed anyone, but this was going to be my first if I expected to live. Afraid to take a breath, I was sweating hard. Even my hands were dripping wet. I wiped my hands on my pants and stayed low, looking between the downed trees, at my back trail. Trying not to make any movement that might be spotted, I waited. It was him or me.

Taking it slow, I got the Spencer ready with the barrel laying on the bottom tree for support. With the brush and trees behind me for cover, whoever was coming would not see me. All I needed was for him to come a few more yards. Trying to remember not to jerk the trigger, I had the sights set in the middle of his chest. He had something hanging around his neck. I saw it moving back and forth, as the horse took each step. As I aimed, I remembered Pa's words about adding a little pressure. And then I felt the rifle slam my shoulder. Quickly, I slammed a new shell into the chamber. When the smoke cleared I saw that the Indian was gone!

His horse was walking back the way he had come. I didn't move. Feeling sick, I fought it down. When I regained control of my stomach, I waited to see if he was alive. Maybe he was looking for me to make the first move.

The minutes passed slowly. There was no sound except the birds. I listened for about thirty minutes, hearing nothing and seeing no movement. I got up real slow. Keeping a tree between me and the place I last saw the Indian, I moved forward. It took at least an hour to creep up to about twenty-five feet of the spot he was last seen.

And then I saw the tip of his foot. He had fallen into a small depression in the ground. He was dead, with a large hole in his chest. His horse was out of sight. The Indian had fallen on top of Pa's Henry. I rolled him over and picked up the Henry. I felt sick a couple of times, but I fought it down again. I had never killed anything other than game, and this was different.

When I returned to my horses, it took at least an hour to get my feelings under control. Trying to remain calm, I picked up my pack and set out for town. As I worked my way down the trail slowly, I watched for any kind of movement, A deer came out of the woods on the other side of the draw. It was looking back, so I eased back into the woods and waited. I did not have long to wait when out of the trees came six braves, riding slowly into the valley. They had about ten horses tied together. It looked like they were heading home after a raid. They were following the tree line as they headed in the other direction from me. Of course, that made me feel a mite better.

I hoped they would stay on the other side of the creek where they would not see my tracks or the fellow I just killed. If they did, they would surely come looking for me. They must not have heard the shot I fired. As I started to breathe again, I moved out, taking my time.

Dark was coming on fast, and I had to find a place to stop for the night. Riding around the point of a ridge, I spotted some willows running down out of the middle of a draw, just ahead about a half-mile. Tying Sally to a tree limb along the small stream, I rode back to the backside of the little ridge. There, I got off and eased up to the top, where I sat a bit, to check for any movement on my back trail. Seeing none, I headed to a spot with taller trees.

Finding a good place in the brush and close to water, I set the picket ropes so the horses could eat and drink. I set up a cold camp, so not to have any smell from a fire. I preferred not to have any company of any kind. I checked the Henry and found it was fully loaded, but the Indian had not been carrying any of the extra shells he had stolen from Pa. It got dark fast when the sun went down and I spent the night rolled up only in my blanket. Without a fire, it was a long cold night.

The sun was lifting over the hills when I opened my eyes. I took my time getting started and just sat there, watching the horses to see if they smelled or heard anything. After a strip of jerky and a drink from the stream, I was ready to head out again. Just before clearing the last trees, I stopped and checked the area. Finding it clear, I clicked Bill with an easy snap of the reins and, with Sally in tow, we headed out. I made better time now, going through less trees and hills.

About noon I topped a small rise and dropped over the other side. I stopped to let the horses eat some bunch grass, while I checked my back trail. From time to time I would ease up the hill and take a look. As luck would have it, there was a small pine tree. I could sit with my back against it, so as not to show myself on the skyline. I was alone.

Late on the second day, I started to see scattered cattle. It was strange because the last time Pa and I made this trip, there was not one cow in the whole area. Riding until the sun was going down, I spotted smoke drifting up among the trees. I took my time to make sure it was a cabin and not a campfire. It pays to be sure. With a little light left, I spotted a cabin that was settled in front of a rock- faced hill. It also had a lean-to shed and pole corrals with some stock inside.

When I got closer, I shouted out to the house - asking if I could come on in. When I got the ok, I moved forward. When I got up closer to the house I saw three rifles pointed at me from behind gun ports in the house. After seeing I was alone, the family inside lowered their guns and had me dismount.

Their son, Little John, came out to lead the horses and me to the corrals. To my relief, he let me fork some hay to Bill and Sally. Picking up my two rifles, I followed Little John to the house. He said his family had been hit by a band of Indians just a few weeks ago, and the Indians had run off with their team. As luck would have it, the family was able to save the saddle stock they had hidden back in a draw behind the house.

Chapter 4 APPLEGATES RANCH

When Sam and Beth Applegate greeted me at the door, they asked about my guns and who I was. I said "Ronnie Campbell."

"What are you doing our here in the wilderness, by yourself?" Sam asked.

"I am alone cuz my Ma died last year, and Pa was killed in an Indian raid a few weeks back."

They seemed like real good folks. They invited me into the cabin and made me feel welcome. Beth said dinner would be on in a jig. "You can go out back and wash up, I'm making Little John do the same." Having a washbasin, towels, and a house got the memories rushing back.

The prospect of good food changed my mood - and man, was I ready to eat. During dinner, the questions flew and most of them were directed at me, about what I was going to do, and how I would survive the winter.

I laid out my plan about selling the two draft horses and getting a saddle horse, along with a packhorse. "So I can carry my winter supplies back to the dugout."

Sam and Beth said they wanted me to stay with them for a few days to think things out. They said I was a mite young to be on my own this far out from anybody.

In the morning when I got up, Sam had Bill and Sally hooked to a wagon. He was hauling in a load of wood that had been cut for the winter, and the splitting still needed to be done. He was in a right good mood because his team had been driven off, and his saddle stock would not fit the harness. I could see that part of my plan had a chance of working. I wanted to sell, or trade, the team for two saddle horses anyway.

I was happy to be of use when Sam called for me and Little John to help unload the wood. After unloading the wagon, lunch was ready, and Sam wanted to talk about what I was going to do with my team. "Well," I said, "Bill and Sally are a really good team and Pa paid top money for them back east."

Sam said to me, "It sounds like your Pop talked to you a little about horse trading from what you have said. Is that right?"

"Well," I said, "Mr. Applegate, I am thinking about selling or trading the team for a horse, saddle and a pack horse. I have a good team, but I have no wagon or harness. You are short two workhorses to fill the harnesses you have, and to pull your wagon. What kind of deal do you think we could come up with for my two horses?"

Mr. Applegate said, "You do know it is hard to get a good saddle horse in this part of the country don't you?"

"Well," I said right back, "look at all of the time you will save just trying to rework all the harness and other stuff to fit your stock horses."

Beth came over and sat down. "Look Ronnie," she said. "Let's do this. You should stay with us for a while. Sam will give you two of our stock horses and a saddle in exchange for the team. We really do need them, and now you need to listen to the rest of this offer. We'd like you to live with us for a year or so and after that you can do what you want. We need another hand to help Little John and Sam with the work around the place. We will give you half wages and keep you in duds.

"What am I to do with the claim and my stuff at the dugout?" I said.

Sam spoke up, "OK, Ronnie, you can go back from time to time to check on things after the Indians calm down a bit. How does that sound?" "Well," I said, "We can give it a try and see if it works, but I do own the two horses and saddle, right Sam?"

Sam said it was a deal and we would put it down on paper, after which he pointed out that I would need a pack frame for my pack horse Joe. "I will show you how to build one," he said. "So let's get to working so Beth will feed us dinner tonight."

The next morning Sam had his team hooked to the wagon and Little John and I were told to go out and check on the cattle. He told us to drive them up into the high meadows in order to save the lower grass for winter. "Take your rifles and keep off the ridges Keep a close watch out for Indians and don't lose sight of each other."

My new mount was called Dandy, and Little John was riding my new packhorse, Joe.

As I found out, Sam had mustang mares and a good Standard Bred stallion back in the hills, just south of the place. He was planning on selling cattle and horses to the military for food and remounts. He had a good start, as he had about twenty mares with the stud.

Little John led the way from the ranch, heading back into the hills north of the house. We were looking for sick or injured cows. I found out darned quick that when it came to roping cows, I had some catching up to do, especially when we found one stuck in the mud.

Little John about fell off his horse watching me catch everything with my rope, except the cow, not once getting the rope over the cow's head. After a bit he dropped the loop over its head and pulled her out.

The next problem was how to get his rope back. It was either get it back, or as he put it, we would run out of ropes really soon. I had to get the rope off its head by throwing the cow to the ground, or having Little John pull it, while I tried to catch its hind feet. In due time, I did get her hind feet. It was more by luck than anything else – but as little John said, "Luck is good." Getting the rope off her head, I then let her walk out of my rope. With two ropes recovered, we were having a good day, and I was learning a lot.

After a few days, I got a mite better. In fact – in just a few days, we could head and heel a cow in short order. On this particular day, the sun was getting high as we started looking for a good spot to eat and look over the area. We found a trail heading up to a bunch of rocks on a ridge. Topping out on the ridge, the trail led us to good grass for the horses. The spot also gave us a good look-see over the entire valley. During our little morning rodeo, we had not noticed any sign of other horses being the area. It was after lunch and we started to move some cattle out of the brush back to better grass and water in the high country,

Dandy could move right well. A few times chasing a cow, he turned so fast I almost went the other way. As we started back to the ranch we decided we had to see who was on the fastest horse. Well, both were about even. But when we reached the corral Sam came out and let us have a what for. "Don't you ever bring in a hot horse and turn it out in my corral, for any reason." He made us walk the horses for a half hour before giving each a good rub down. After cleaning and brushing both horses, they just walked out and rolled in the mud. "Thanks," we both said heading in for dinner.

All summer, we kept watch on the cattle - moving them from one meadow to another and every once in a while, pulling a cow or two out of the mud. Time was moving along.

When we had any free time Sam asked us, "How about we split some of that wood I cut?"

It seemed like he would never quit cutting the blocks to split. Then with the weather cooling off, Sam sent us out to move the cattle down out of the high country. When we had that done, we started cutting grass hay for the horses.

We also split the wood as Sam hauled it in. We needed a lot to cover the cold weather that was coming soon. I didn't think Sam would ever quit having us boys split wood, and it did put some muscle on my bones.

When Sam figured it was time to get some of the two year olds started, Little John and I began training horses. After about a month of breaking horses, we began to stay aboard, instead of sitting on the ground.

Breeding the mustang mares to the Standard Bred stud was working. This bunch could really run. I soon found out that the two year olds were much faster than either Dandy or Joe and I had my eye on one of the largest of the horses. He was built a lot like the stud. Just a little bit shorter but he was heavier in the shoulders.

I worked on him more than the others, and he was quick to learn. When I felt the time was right, I was just about ready to ask Sam if I could trade back Joe. I decided I would offer to work for free for the difference.

Sam had an idea of what I was thinking. With a smile he said, "Well Ronnie, you seem to have taken to that young stud".

I told Sam, "I'd like to make a deal for him."

Sam said, "I need to get him out of the herd. If I don't, the stallion will kill or hurt him. Would you like to trade up a little?"

How does a young boy keep from jumping up and down with that offer? But I remembered Pa telling me to keep it cool and let the other one talk a little. It was all I could do, but after a bit, I said. "I don't have much to trade but my time. I could work off the difference." When Sam got quiet, I got nervous. "I do have a couple of gold nuggets," I added. "Pa found them some time back. He was keeping them for hard times."

Old Sam just sat there thinking for a bit, then he came back, "Well, how many of those do you have?"

"Pa had three that had some size to them," I said, adding, "I could trade them for the difference if you could use them at the store in town.

Old Sam was still just sitting there thinking. After a bit he asked if he could have a look at them. Remembering what Pa had said about planning ahead, I had, by chance, separated some of the nuggets I found in the small stream. I told him Pa had found them. I reached into my pocket and pulled out three of the four and showed them to him. I had kept the largest for myself.

I could see that Old Sam was thinking how he could pay down the bill at the store and have a little cash on top of that. He said right quick, "Do you have any more gold?"

I said, "No, not any to amount to anything. Pa used what he had to pay down his bill. There is just a little dust left. As I said before these nuggets were what Pa had kept back for hard times."

After sitting a bit longer, Sam picked up the three nuggets and said, "We got a deal. I'll take back Joe and you can keep the young stud."

It was all I could do - to not jump for joy, but I played it down. I got up, went outside and saddled my new stud colt to take a ride. Then I would find a quiet spot and yell for joy. I decided to call the young stud Diamond, because of the diamond on his forehead.

After working on the ranch all summer, I asked Sam if I could go back to the claim and check things out. He said it would be ok to take a few days but I needed to keep a sharp eye out for danger. The next day Dandy was loaded with supplies and Diamond was ready to hit the trail.

Little John wanted to go, but I told him he should stay and get some more wood split while I was gone. (Just what every young kid wants to hear!) After breakfast, he got me. "I should stomp you into a mud hole for setting me up to split more wood," he said.

"You need to have something to do while I am gone," I smiled.

Before I left, Sam had made a trip to town, so now I had a full box of shells for the Henry. Unknown to him, I fingered the gold nugget that I kept for myself. It was in my pocket. Thinking about what I would do when I got there, I had a mind to look over the little stream where I found the nugget to see if there was any more.

I made good time the first day. That night, I made a cold camp just to be safe. The next morning I climbed up to a good spot to look around when the sun was just rising over the hills. After about thirty minutes I saw no smoke and felt that I could move on - keeping to the low ground and back in the trees a bit.

Noon found me looking at some of my old hunting grounds. Now was the time to really keep a good eye out for trouble. So far, I saw no tracks at any of the stream crossings. I did not use the regular crossings but stayed up stream a bit - off to the side of the trail. At one place, I doubled back to see if anything or anybody had been around. Finding nothing, I started to feel better.

The sun was getting low, so I moved on, planning to make the dugout by dark. As I rode along, I wondered if my stuff was still there, or if the Indians had come and cleaned me out. If I had what I left - and what I had packed on Dandy - I knew I could make out for a few weeks. When I got to the dugout and found everything as I left it, I felt much better. I even thought I might be able to get some sleep tonight.

I chanced a small fire in the old stove and made some pan biscuits. I also fried up a little bacon and made some coffee. It tasted mighty good. That night I got up often, to check on the horses. All seemed ok, so I went back to bed. Just as it was getting light, I got up and walked out, with the Henry loaded and ready if needed. I was sitting on a high bank for a while, watching for any sign of Indians, when out of the trees came a real nice buck heading to water. It was a temptation! I could use the meat, but I wanted to keep things quiet around the claim. So I decided the buck could wait for another day.

Chapter 5 FINDING MY BANK

As a kid will do, when letting his mind wander, the idea of gold had me thinking about a lot of stuff. In my mind, I was buying everything I had ever seen and wanted. The only problem was I didn't have any of the gold yet, and besides I was just fifteen years old. I didn't feel any different than I felt before my birthday – and I never told Beth, Sam or even Little John that I was a year older. It just never came up

Thinking about that kind of stuff could get me pretty wound up. Now back on Pa's claim, I put Dandy on a picket by the water where he had plenty of grass to eat. Diamond and I headed off to the little stream where I found the first nugget.

We made good time and were about there by mid morning. Finding a good spot to picket Diamond, I started to walk the stream looking for some sign of gold. Working slowly along the water, I found another nugget alongside a rock that was half out of the water. I was seeing more color than Pa and I ever found before. Finding a few more nuggets, I was getting closer to owning that new Navy Colt. I spent most of the morning looking around the area and working up to higher ground, looking to see if a vein would show itself. The sun was getting high when I headed back down to Diamond. I took it slow and stopped every so often to take a look around.

After a bit of jerky, I got the pan and started sampling the stream. Not every pan had gold, but it was way better than the area Pa and I had worked before. I think this was what Pa had been looking to find. I worked the rest of the day panning and finding some good nuggets - along with some gold flakes.

Finding the gold in this new stream was great and I realized that trading three nuggets for Diamond was the best deal I could have ever made. I was thinking I found a real pocket. With this amount of gold, I needed to keep it quiet, but yet be able to spend some of it on the new Colt pistol I wanted. I headed back to camp at a fair pace, taking a different way after removing any sign of being in the area.

I could see that I was going to have to keep my find a secret until I could file a proper claim. Or maybe I might just come back and work the stream to build up cash for whenever I needed more money. This could be my bank when I needed to buy something important.

After getting back to the dugout, I set about to improve the place. Now I was thinking about the gold and what I wanted to do with Pa's claim. After working with Sam and Beth, I could also see that this place could work as a good cattle range. I might be able to file on a large chunk of it. If I did this, I could keep anyone from finding the gold. I needed to think on it for a few days, but, first of all, I would have to scout the area to mark off the land and water needed to make a paying ranch. I planned to ask Sam how he filed on his land. He might help me do the paper work. My other concern was I didn't know how old I had to be to file a claim.

Over the next few days, I pushed Diamond and Dandy to the limit, riding out and making a map of the land I wanted. I had to get back soon, or Sam would come looking for me. After a week out, I packed up and headed back to the Applegate's ranch - and back to the day-to-day operations that I needed to learn how to manage for when I set up my own ranch. Having a plan in place, I decided to study why Sam did things the way he did them. Sam was a willing talker, and the more he talked, the better my plan was forming up in my mind.

I asked him one day, "Why did you get the Standard Bred stallion?" This was heavy on my mind.

"Well," Sam said, "he was free."

"How did you come by that deal?" I asked, amazed.

"Well," he said, "The army wanted better horses so they will give a rancher a stallion, and by breeding the mustang mares to him, I got a better ride and more speed. Diamond is one of the first colts out of the stud. I think you have tested him out and can see what a difference the breeding makes. Dandy and Joe are mustangs, and they lack the speed you get from the stallion, but remember the mustang mares make a horse that can eat anything and do well on a long patrol, even if they only eat bunch grass."

It was stuff I needed to know, and Sam figured I was just trying to do a good job. As I learned, Sam worked on some large ranches in his past. One of the most important things he said he learned was how to work with the young horses, how to get their trust and then bring them along slowly.

And soon, fall worked into winter. We had some snow and rain for a few weeks. "It's time to finish training the horses" Sam said.

He had had a bit of fun with us on the first couple of horses we started. He let us get bucked off and kicked a few times before giving us some pointers. He told us to watch the lead mare in the herd. She kept the other horses in line. In order to do it, she would just keep facing the offender and move him out of the herd. It caused the young studs a lot of stress. Sam told me to watch when she turned to the side, "Watch the young studs pick up their heads, move over and make up to her."

When we started to train a young horse, we put it in the round pen and forced it to walk, trot, and run around by using the rope – as we stood in front of it and faced it down. After a while, they would drop their heads and start chewing. That was the time to turn away. Then the horse would come over and allow us to touch it. After this, we could move along much faster, getting them to accept our training since we now had their trust. By using this method, we were able to handle their feet and not get kicked. It took a few hours instead of days.

Then Sam told Little John to bring in a couple of steers and put them in the pen next to the round corral where we worked the young horses. As we advanced the training to handling steers, Sam asked us how the horses were doing when roping and holding a calf – how they behaved when we got off to check the steer out. We told him that it took both of us to catch a calf.

Sam said, "Here, I'm gonna show you a trick. You need to have your horse watch the calf or steer when you have a rope on it. Bring one of the young horses over to the round pen, so I can show you how to do it."

He was tricky; he put the loop over the horns of the steer and ran the rope through the fence and into the round pen. Now Sam had us put a halter on the colt. He ran the rope through the halter and tied the rope off to the saddle horn. Then he turned the steer loose and the fun came when he dumped some feed into the feed box, along with some water into the tank. That's when, as the steer started to go to the food, it about pulled the horse over.

It didn't take very long before the horse wouldn't take his eyes off the steer. We kept this up for a couple of days. Then we went out and roped a steer, and when it was caught, the horse just kept pulling back to help keep the rope tight. Now we could hold a calf with just one of us.

The winter was on us, full force at the first of the year, so we had plenty of tack repairs to keep us busy. We were looking at 1860 - hoping it would be a better year than the old one.

Sitting around the stove for a few weeks, I questioned Sam about how he got this land - what it cost - things Pa had talked about from time to time. Sam told me he made a map on paper, and this map had land marks called out on it to show what he owned. "You remember seeing the pile of rock on top of the mountain with the broken snag on it, don't you?"

"Yeah," I said, "That is about 5 miles south of here."

"Well," Sam said, "It is one of my markers that shows my southeast corner. I just rode out in four different directions and placed landmarks that are my corner markers.

Another thing I did was to take land that would block anyone else from using it. If I have the water they can't pass through my land to get to what they want and I can use it for my cattle. I had my corner markers set down on paper and I marked the streams. Then I had to get it on file at the land office."

Sam and Beth were good people, but I had a mind not to tell them much. I was thinking if they had any idea what I wanted to do, they might think hard on the gold I had used to get Diamond. Gold causes people to do things they would never normally do so I kept the location of the gold to myself - just like Pa said.

Winter was easing up and we moved the cattle to put them on better feed in the lower valleys. It was warming up and spring was on the way. The time had come for me to go into town. I had about grown out of all my clothes. My boots were down to nubs and my shirts had moved up my arms so they were hard to button.

One night at dinner I made my needs known. I had a plan and I needed to get started. Sam said he was planning to go to town in a few weeks, and added, "But if you want to go now, it's okay. It's up to you. You could go with me, if you wait."

"I'll go now," I said. "As you can see, I'm growing out of my duds."

Beth said, "You are mite young to be traipsing around alone. You need to keep low and stay out of trouble."

"I'll be careful," I promised.

This is Dandy. He has carried the mail the last two years for the Pony Express re-ride. We have covered a part of the trail from the power plant out by Sand Mountain east to the power lines. This is just over seven miles.

Photo by Nick McCabe

Chapter 6 FINDING A FRIEND

That night I got ready for my trip to town. I got out both of my rifles. Sam said, "You planning on going to war?"

"You never know," I said.

The next morning light was just showing over the mountains when I saddled Diamond. I had already put the packsaddle on Dandy and he was ready. Picking up the lead rope and sliding the Henry into the boot, I clicked Diamond into a shuffle-foot trot and we were off. It was still cold and snow remained in some shady spots. As for staying warm, my coat was way too small. I had put on some weight and filled out a bit. Yes, I was ready for new duds.

After leaving the homestead I made good time but was watchful at the same time. I moved through some broken hills and had just stopped to water the horses in a small stream when I heard a shot. Out of a draw, to my right and downstream, came a rider running flat out. I saw him turn around and take a shot behind him. It didn't take long to see he had six braves on his tail.

They couldn't see me because the brush along the creek had me covered. Having to make a quick decision, my first thought was to hole up and wait it out. However, seeing that it was six to one, I decided to give chase, to see if I could make a difference. Picking up the reins, I stepped into the saddle and put the spurs to Diamond.

In about three jumps, he was pulling Dandy along. Dropping the lead rope, I let Diamond have his head and we were running flat out. Gaining fast; I had the Spencer out, ready to shoot. I saw the fleeing rider fire his pistol and knock one of the Indians off his horse.

I could see he was dead because he was not moving. Now there were five, and only one Indian had a rifle. Riding hard, I was getting in range, but I held my fire. Diamond and I were closing in fast from behind, and on the Indian's left side. I was ready to shoot when the fleeing rider's horse was hit. He went down and out of sight. Riding full out, I was coming up behind the Indian with the rifle. When he heard me, he started to swing around to take a shot at me. I pulled the trigger and down he went. The other four turned off hard to the right. I fired the next six rounds without hitting any of them. They were already off about a hundred yards.

Seeing I was out of bullets, they turned and headed back to get me. I checked Diamond at the edge of the bank and slid down to the bottom. The other rider was there, but his horse was on top of his leg, and he was trapped. I dropped the Spencer and pulled the Henry out of the boot and climbed up the bank.

It didn't look good. Four Indians were coming in hard, so I levered a round into the Henry's chamber and fired. I hit one brave in the right shoulder. He dropped down over his horse's neck and pulled back into the trees. I let off five more shots and got two more down. The last brave turned back, heading for cover in the trees, leaving a couple of horses loose in the sage brush.

"Amigo, can you get me out from under this horse?" the downed rider asked.

I managed to pull him clear of the dead horse, after a bit of swearing on his part. Pulling his rifle out of his scabbard, he limped up the bank to take a look at the damage. As far as we could tell, the wounded Indian and the one I missed, were hightailing it home. "I don't see any sign of them"," I said. Then I asked, "Can you get along for a bit?"

When he said he could, I went back to pick up my packhorse, Dandy, only to see he was coming along on his own: It was like he was missing Diamond and me. I saw that the lead rope was a problem. With every step he took, he stepped on the rope. I swung in, picked it up, and we headed back to the downed rider. I also gathered the loose horses and brought them along. For sure, the rider was going to need one of them.

Leading Dandy and the two Indian ponies, Diamond and I slid back down into the wash. My new friend had his saddle off the dead horse. He was glad to have a ride, even if the two Indian ponies I caught would not make up for the one he lost. It looked like the dead horse was a real fine one.

I slipped off the saddle and said, "My name is Ronnie Campbell."

He came back with, "Juan Lopez is mine."

"Maybe you can put your saddle on one of these ponies," I said, "and we'll find a safe spot where we can make a fire and have some coffee."

Juan joked that he thought I could use a little time to stop my hands from shaking – even though I was trying to hide how worked up I was. Then he added, "Thanks. If you had not showed up, I'd dead now, and the Indians would be eating my horse."

We didn't stay there long. We mounted the horses and worked our way downstream, where we found a sheltered spot with some boulders and trees. At the backside was a rock wall; a good spot to take a rest.

It was getting along in the day, so with water and grass for the horses, we could sit back and talk as we fixed dinner. Juan said he was looking for a job when he got jumped by the Indians. His wife and two kids were waiting for him to find a ranch that would put him to work.

He was down in the mouth about his horse. Now he was without, what he called, a good cutting horse. He was older than me by a few years, and he had been around a bit more that me. As we sat around the fire, talking, he told me he had been working for a ranch, but the owner got killed, and his wife was trying to sell the stock so she could move back east.

I asked if he could read and write and he answered, "Yes, I have been schooled some."

"Well," I told him, "My Ma and Pa both worked with me on my schooling. We had some books and they made me read." I told him about the Indian attack on our place and how Pa was killed. I also said, "I miss the books and my folks."

Juan's leg was going to be okay – even if it was a little sore. We sat up late and talked about sleeping light. I brought Diamond up close to my bedroll. If anyone might come near us, he would blow and wake me up.

We were so tired, I don't think either of us could have heard anything. In the morning, we both woke with a start. Luck was with us. The horses were cropping grass. I asked Juan to start the fire while I took them to water. After setting the picket pins in a new location on new grass, I went back to the fire. Juan had bacon in the pan and we had a few biscuits left so we were able to eat just fine. Life is good when you have some bacon to slap on a biscuit and are able to wipe up the grease with another biscuit. During the night I had got to thinking about the ranch and the things I needed to do. Juan was twenty-five years old, with two kids and a wife and no place to go. I was fifteen, with an idea, and I needed help. This could be a good thing for both of us.

Juan was just about to saddle up so we could get started, when I said, "Let's set a mite and talk. I have a problem you might be able to help me with, being that you owe me a little for saving your bacon and all."

Juan just gave me a look that said, "What do you need?"

I said, "I have an idea that could work to both of our advantages if we can work it out. We have some food left, so let's just sit back and talk."

"Go ahead," he answered.

"My idea is this! You and I may just be what each is looking for. Let me tell you how I think we could work out a job for you, and I get my ranch at the same time. I am a mite young to march in and file on the property I want to file on. (I was mindful of not getting the gold involved in any way.)

Juan said, "Ronnie, the way you handled your gun on them Indians, I would not want to cross you. You may be young but you are one tough guy. I saw that for sure!"

"I did what I needed to do at the time, Juan. Now, this is what I think I should do. I have scouted out a good ranch with water and plenty of grass. After working for Sam and Beth Applegate, I decided to run some cattle and raise horses on my own place, and I have found that place. What do you think about that?" I asked.

Juan answered with a question: "Well, how do you plan to pay for the seed stock and get the rest of the startup money?"

I said, "My folks had a little money set aside. Now that they are gone, it is mine to do with what I want. How many head of cattle does the lady you were working for have to sell?"

"About four hundred head of mixed stock. She had some young bulls and of the four hundred cows, there were about one hundred fifty young stock.

"Could we go and buy the herd, sell off the older stock and drive the young stuff over here?"

Juan gave me a surprised look.

"The money we get for the older stock," I said, "will help pay for needed startup supplies. Maybe that woman would be willing to sell her wagon and other things, for a good price, just so she can get on her way. Juan, do you think you could hire some help to get this job done?"

Juan answered, "I have a little brother at home with my wife and kids. He is your age and can work cattle. My wife Juanita can ride. She can be our cook on the trail. The little ones can ride in the wagon."

We talked for the rest of the day and into the night about how to get my ranch started. I was thinking, if Juan could help me with this, I would cut him in for a piece of the ranch later on. But first, I decided to wait and see how things worked out.

Plan in place, we headed into town for supplies; and to see if we could get my land filed on - proper like. When we got into town I told Juan, "Those two horses we picked up – you can have them. You can do whatever you want with them."

Later that day, he was riding a better horse. It was not his trained cutting horse, but it was a start. After that, Juan asked around and found the land office in town. There, Juan said he was filing for me because my Pa was sick and could not make it into town himself. With my drawing and help from Juan, we got it done.

Chapter 7 CATTLE FOR MY RANCH

Now I had a new problem. Sam was expecting me back in a week or so, and I didn't want to ride back to their ranch before going to get my ranch stock. The best I could do was leave a message with Mr. Brown at the general store. He would tell Sam that I was okay and was going on a cattle drive. I'd be back in a month or so.

And now, it sure felt good to have new clothes that fit - and a new hat. Juan was happy too. His horse was better than it looked. He had good feet and could move out and cover ground, even if there was no way he could keep up with Diamond on a hard run. The blacksmith did have a little trouble shoeing Diamond and Dandy. It was the first time they had their feet worked on, other than being trimmed.

When Dandy was loaded with supplies to last a couple of weeks, Juan and I set out to meet the widow Betty Smith and make a cattle deal. We had no way of knowing if she had sold out yet or not; we just went on faith that we could make a deal.

I remember coming this way with Ma and Pa - what seemed like a lifetime ago – and still only a little under two years ago. A lot of things had changed since then. Since I lost both of them, I lived with another family for a time. Then I found the gold Pa had been looking for and now, I was on my way to start a ranch.

With Juan being the guide, we had stopped at a couple of trading posts, along the way, where I saw posters saying, *Ride for the Pony Express.* It sounded like a lot of fun, ride fast horses and get paid for the fun. We were on the trail for a week before Juan turned off, heading back into the hills. We rode all that day, skirting some hills. It was getting late when we make camp. After having some dinner Juan said, "By early morning, we will be getting into the valley where the ranch is."

As I was thinking how I was going to handle the payment for the cattle and equipment, I remembered something that Pa said. "Don't show your cards on the first hand". Without Juan knowing it, I had taken the gold and divided it up into smaller bags. I had it valued when we were in town. Juan never knew that I was packing gold. I'm sure he never spent any time thinking on it. I had put half of the gold dust in the bank and had a draft I could make out for up to $8,000.00 to pay the widow Mrs. Smith with. I had a slight suspicion she may take less, if it was gold. Just maybe the widow would like to put the gold in her bags and ride off in her buggy.

Juan was right. We rode in about mid-morning, where his wife Juanita, kids little Juan and Hector, and Tony his younger brother greeted us. They were happy to see him home alive. The widow Betty Smith was pleased as well, asking about his trip to find work.

That's when Juan introduced me. "This is Ronnie. He came with me, because he wants to make a deal with you for cattle and equipment. He also offered me a job on his ranch."

She looked at me, a little puzzled. "Do you have any money?" she said.

"Well, both my folks died. Indians killed my Pa. He did leave me a little money and if your price is ok, I might buy everything you have. Juan said that you want to go back east."

She smiled, "Well, Ronnie, that's very interesting."

"But first I need to take a look at your equipment and stock," I said, before adding that I would need to drive the stock to market and sell the older cows, so I could finish paying her the balance.

We spent most of the day with her, looking at what she had around the cabin. She told me how good her stock was and I spent my negotiating time telling her about all of the work I would need to do, just to get the stock back to my ranch.

The next day Juan and I rode out to look over the cattle she had. Juan was right. She had about one hundred fifty head of young stock that I could use. The rest could go to market.

When I tried to make a deal, Mrs. Smith wanted more than I wanted to pay. Therefore, I made a strategic move and told Juan we should be getting his household items ready to travel. I acted like it was all over – like I needed to go into town and pick up a wagon to haul Juan's belongings along with his family back to my ranch. It was surely what Pa would have said to get things moving along on making a deal. Pa had said that some times the best deal is made when you are about to walk away from it. On the third day, after lunch, with me planning on moving out in the morning, the widow lowered her price, accepting the amount I wanted to pay.

We sat in the kitchen drinking coffee and when the deal was made for the draft. I said, "Would you take less if I paid you in gold?" That's when she almost dropped her coffee cup. "You can keep your buggy," I added, "and the light team to pull it. Then you can go into town, sell them for whatever price you can get. I think that adds up to a bit more."

Her eyes were big and I could see it might have pleased her, but then I had one concern. I said, "Please do not tell Juan or anyone else that I paid in gold. It could cause both of us problems."

She accepted the deal and when I gave her two ten pound bags with ten or so gold nuggets, it added up to about seven thousand dollars for the whole operation. I advised her, "Mrs. Smith, if you need additional money after what you get from your buggy and horses, you can trade the nuggets for cash at the first bank you come to on the stage line."

All this was coming from a fifteen-year old kid, but still she listened. "Like my Pa told me, I'd advise you - don't cash in any of the gold until you get back east. And then to be on the safe side - don't deposit it in only one bank. If it's possible, take little trips to different cities and make deposits in different banks. If you put the gold in only one bank, it might cause people to think you have more hidden in your house and they will come looking for it.

*

As soon as Widow Smith was on the road – Juan, his brother and I gathered the herd. The wagon was loaded with ranch equipment and Juan's stuff and we started the cattle drive to town. When we got there, we took the livestock to the stock pens and sorted the herd. By the time we finished it, we had a couple of cattle buyers looking on. Now I sat back and let Juan talk. He told the buyers that my pa sent us down with this bunch to sell. After we told them how good the cattle were, they told us they were a little short on weight. After some wrangling, we came to a deal for twenty-five dollars a head. This was for the two hundred and fifty older stock-just about what I paid for the four hundred head in all.

Hoof Beats Sounding on the Old Pony Express Trail

Photo by Nick McCabe

Chapter 8 CATTLE DRIVE

While Juan and I were finishing up with selling the cattle, Juanita was down at the store, ordering supplies for the trip to my newly deeded ranch. As soon as the cash deal was made, Juan and I drifted down to the store to load our supplies into the wagon. That's when I noticed that Jonas, the owner of the store, had one new Henry rifle and a Navy Colt on the rack.

I negotiated with him for a long time, trying to make a deal for both the rifle and pistol. Just as Juan and I were ready to go, Jonas called me back to talk one last time. When it was finished, I had a new Henry, along with 1000 rounds, and 500 extra rounds for the Spencer. I paid a little extra for ball and powder for the pistols. With all the money I had made, I was able to pay for the supplies; with plenty left over to start building up the ranch.

On the front door of the store, I saw another poster advertising to hire young orphans who are slight of build – to ride for the Pony Express. Not quite sure that I might be considered slight; I did feel that I was a good rider. I decided to look into it when I got to Mr. Brown's Store. It sounded like fun.

Once the wagon was loaded, I got us all a hot meal and a room for the night. We all needed to clean up, and it was my first time, ever, taking a bath in a big old copper tub. For Juan and his family, I think it was their first time as well. The next morning, as the sun was climbing over the hills, we had our last meal in town. As we ate, I said, "We better enjoy it cuz it may be awhile to the next one."

And there was one last thing I had to do before we left town. I had to make a deal for at least six stock horses to get us back to the ranch. I was in luck. I heard about a man who had some brood mares for sale. He was making a move into town and wanted to sell. All of the mares had been working stock, so we made a deal that included a couple of extra saddles because they came with the horses. Juan's brother, Tony, now had a horse he could move the cattle with. It was important that, as we traveled, we could change horses at noon each day to keep them fresh.

Opening the gate to the stock pens and moving out the young stock was when I realized that, now, I was in the cattle business. Juan still didn't know that he would get part of the ranch. I was keeping it under my hat until the proper time came along. When Juan moved the last of the young stock out of the pens, I called him over and handed him the new Henry. "Give the old Spencer to Tony," I said.

Juan said, "Thanks. This just may come in handy."

Driving cattle takes experience. Starting out, we went slow for a bit, waiting for one of the herd to step out to take the lead. When that happened we could start making better time. We moved the herd slowly for a couple of hours; having to push cows back into the herd, many wanted to go back where they came from. Just before noon, one of the young bulls moved to the front and pointed his nose west. We had our leader.

Juan had Juanita moved the wagon to the front to keep it out of the dust. We set the pace, and the lead bull was leading the cattle. As I rode along, I reflected that before the time comes to offer Juan a part of the ranch, I needed him to show me if he could be a leader. Today he was doing it. As we moved closer to Mr. Brown's store, he had things under control.

I knew that it would take a few years to get the young stock into a herd of any size. If I went to ride for Pony Express, Juan and Tony would have to manage the ranch. They had experience working cattle, as they proved when we got the herd moving along without much trouble. For now, Juanita was in the lead with the wagon and the little kids. As kids do, they were having fun, watching us come along behind. Juan and I rode on each side of the small herd, while Tony rode in the drag. We were on our way home.

With the extra horses I purchased, I let Diamond out to run with the remuda I could see that Diamond figured by the time we get back to the ranch, he would have all of the mares in foal.

To be safe, each night we set up a watch. It was nice to have a cook on the trail, and Juanita sure could cook. If this was going to keep up, I would need larger pants soon. Even Little Juan and Hector were pulling their weight by picking up fire wood and helping around camp each night.

We were on the trail for about two weeks when, about noon, two riders came up to the herd and stopped short of the wagon. Tony and I rode up one on each side. Juanita pulled out her Spencer and had it ready if needed. Tony and I had them out flanked, and they seemed nervous about that.

The rider on my side said, "We are going to take ten head as payment for crossing our land."

"What makes you think you own this land?"

"Because I said so" was his reply!

Right then, Juan came out of the trees behind them and levered a round into the chamber of his new Henry rifle. The strangers heard it and neither of them dared to take a look, but they sure wanted to. "Well gents," I said, "The only ground you will own is the ground we dig the hole in to plant you. Now, shuck your guns real slow and let them fall."

The gunman on Tony's side did not want to drop his pistol. The one on my side did as I told him to. Seeing it, the other one soon followed. With their pistols on the ground, I said, "Now pull out your rifles and let them fall. If you don't, I will own two new horses."

"Look, we were just funning you," the talkative one said. "And now, we'll just be on our way."

"Yes, you may be on your way," I said, "but you will not have any guns, and if you keep talking, you will be walking. Now move! I thumbed back the hammer on the Henry,

Tony had his Spencer pointed at the two. The man on the right got the point and started getting rid of his iron, the second one soon followed. With the guns on the ground, I said, "Now you can go."

"You are going to get us killed without any guns," the mouthy one said.

"If you make it alive to the next town, you might want to think on your harsh ways. Maybe you will be a bit more sociable from now on."

Tony stepped down to pick up the guns and put them in the wagon. Juanita put the Spencer back and clicked up the horses as we resumed our trip to Mr. Brown's store.

After getting rid of the herd cutters, we drove the herd late to put some miles between the bad men and the herd. I rode on ahead to scout out a good camping spot for the night, along a small seep coming out of a canyon that led north. The cattle would have plenty of grass to graze on so they would not be hard to hold close to camp. As I started to turn back to the herd I spotted some wild horses drinking upstream a bit.

I started back down the trail and saw Juanita was just off a short way. I told her to drive the wagon. Juan came up and turned the cattle off a bit from the wagon and moved them up to the water to drink. After the cattle were watered and starting to graze, they settled in. They would eat for a few hours then lay down and rest.

Let's see if Juanita has some coffee ready, we need to talk about having some fun" I said. With coffee in hand and sitting on some large rocks along the small stream I laid out a plan. "Look guys, I just spotted some mustangs being led by a bay stallion. Some of the mares are better than average. I think the stallion has a few too many mares for his own good."

"I will go out and see where they bed down for the night, then about an hour before light we will slip into position and try to cut out some the mares. We can drive them back here to our remuda and let Diamond take over. They will follow a stallion without much trouble. What do you think?"

With plans made, Ronnie asked Juanita if she could use a day of rest just staying around camp. She said that it would be great to be able to catch up on mending and play with the kids.

It was late when Ronnie came back from scouting the wild horses. He stopped to talk to Juan who had the first watch riding night herd on the cattle. Ronnie would take the watch from 2 until he got the others up to make the raid on the stallion's mares. Tony woke Ronnie up for his watch and went to bed to get a few hours of sleep before the raid.

It was a dark night so it was hard to see when Tony and Juan saddled up their horses. Juanita had set aside some food for them to eat on the way so not to lose any time. Ronnie led the way out into the dark. He was mounted on Diamond. He wanted the best and would need a horse that could outrun the stallion so he could split the herd.

Diamond was hard to hold back because he had not been worked for a few weeks. After a bit he settled down to an easy trot, Ronnie held this pace until they got to within a mile of the herd's location. Then they would need to walk. Reaching a small hill, Ronnie dropped down to a walk. As he was about to reach the top of the hill he stepped off Diamond and ground tied him. Juan and Tony did the same. Looking over the hill they could see the horses had not moved to water yet.

The plan was for Ronnie to slip north behind the hill they were looking over and get a little ahead of the herd. When the sun started over the ridge on the east side of the horses, Juan and Tony would split up. Juan would take the far side of the horse herd and Tony would drop down from his location and take up his position. Ronnie would ride hard at the stallion to push the herd back to Juan and Tony.

The first rays of the sun were slicing over the ridge when Ronnie moved Diamond out at a trot heading right at the stallion. Ronnie was about a half mile from the herd when the stallion raised his head and snorted, getting his mares up and moving away. He had only gone a few hundred yards when he saw Juan and Tony on each side of his herd. With a squeal he pushed the mares back toward Ronnie.

Ronnie put the spurs to Diamond, heading him just behind the stallion to cut off the mares from him. Juan and Tony had closed the gap and were moving in fast on each flank. Ronnie pulled his 44 Colt and started firing into the ground. The stallion flashed by but Ronnie had already split the mares away from the stallion. Juan and Tony had closed off the flanks so the herd turned back down the canyon. While waiting on the hill they had picked out the eight or ten mares they wanted so as they moved the herd down the valley they let some slip out the sides so they could rejoin the stallion. After a run of about two miles the mares were willing to walk, Ronnie kept the pressure on them and Juan and Tony kept letting the horses they did not want to keep slip around them to rejoin the others behind them.

Now with only the horses they wanted, they pushed them down the canyon. It would take a while to move the mustangs back to their camp to join the remuda. About a mile from camp, Ronnie got off Diamond and turned him loose to join the eight mustang mares they had captured. Diamond would take charge and move them to his herd at camp. Juan would bring Ronnie a fresh horse from back at camp.

After about an hour Juan came back with a horse. Ronnie saddled up and they headed back to camp. When they got there, Diamond had taken charge and was driving the whole herd around, letting everyone know he was the boss.

Ronnie said "let's lay in for a bit in the morning. That will give Diamond a chance to get the new mares settled before we hit the trail."

Juanita was baking some biscuits and frying bacon just after the sun had came over the hills. Who could sleep in with that smell? All were up and ready for the hot coffee and breakfast. (Who needed extra sleep anyway?)

Our little cattle drive was getting closer to home by the fourth week away, if you could say a dugout was a home. I had Juan warn Juanita about the living conditions. Until we got a shelter built, she and the kids would sleep in or under the wagon.

After we got the cattle on the home range, we would start getting some timber down to build a cabin. Juan asked how I wanted the cabin built. With a bit of discussion it was decided it would have two bedrooms, with the kitchen in the large front room. We also decided to build a large stone fireplace at one end of that main room, close to the kitchen. I told Juanita about my old burnt stove, and she said, "For now it will work just fine."

Chapter 9 RIDE THE PONY EXPRESS

When the herd got close to town, I sent Juanita and the wagon in for supplies. Winter was on its way and the air was getting colder by the day. Deciding I'd better help Juanita find what we needed, I left Juan and Tony with the cattle that would be coming along behind. Juanita had a little lead but I did catch her by the time she got to the store.

When I walked in, Jim said, "Sam was here a few weeks back and he asked about you. I told him you were on a cattle drive and would be back after a bit."

Mr. Brown was helping Juanita with our new supplies, while Hector and little Juan were sitting on the store's front step waiting to start home. When I noticed them, I told Mr. Brown, "How come the kids have empty hands?"

He gave me a grin and picked out a stick of candy for each of them. "Now they have something to do," I said.

When the wagon was loaded with everything we needed, Juanita left to drive back to the herd. I stayed to talk to Jim Brown. "I'd like you to let Juan and Juanita have what they need to keep the ranch going." I gave him some money to cover future expenses until I got back.

Jim Brown was a bit puzzled. He said, "What are you planning to do? You just got back and now you have cattle to look after?"

"Well," I said. "I filed on my Pa's land, and also got some cows to raise. Once I get them settled, I am going to talk to the Pony Express. I'm thinking about riding for them."

"Well, just in case you didn't know it, the man who got the Pony Express started, Mr. Russell is going to be in the next town south of here about a day's ride. He'll be arriving there in about a week or so. At least that's what I heard. But I thought you were starting a ranch."

"It's gonna take a while to get it started," I said, "and the Lopez's are going to handle that for me. They will have to work fast at building the cabin to beat the snow.

When we left the store, Juan and Tony had turned the cattle north, to head for Sam and Beth's ranch. Juanita was a good hand with the wagon, and we moved right along with the young bull marching behind, leading the herd. In fact all Juanita had to do was follow the wagon tracks that Sam left when he came to town.

Before reaching Sam & Beth's ranch on the second day, Juan, Tony, and I moved the cattle into a small box canyon just south of the ranch house, Tony said, "I will stay with the cattle to get them settled, and make sure they get water and grass, but I will show up for dinner. The cattle will be ready to move out at first light."

Sam, Beth, and Little John met us as we came to their place. They had lots of questions. "We were worried you might be dead."

"As you can see, I am alive and well." Then I told them, "I filed on the land around the old camp and now I am in the cattle business." Of course the Applegate's looked quite surprised, and I added, "Juan and his family are going to be living on the ranch and taking care of the stock. Tony is with the cattle right now, getting them settled and ready to head out at first light. I also told Sam that I picked up some mares and would like to show them to him on the way out in the morning.

"Let's do it now," he replied. "We can let the women talk and fix dinner, we can go meet Tony."

It sounded good to me. Regarding the women, Beth was older than Juanita but they seemed to get along just fine. I could see it would be nice for Juanita to have someone to visit with, within a couple day's ride from time to time.

From the ranch, I led the way back down to the box canyon where I introduced Tony to Sam and Little John. Tony and Little John were close to the same age. When Sam saw the mares, he said, "Boy you made a good deal! They are fine stock. Maybe, in time, we can swap some horse flesh. Your Pa damned sure turned you into a pretty good horse trader."

"Now what about the other eight mares you have?" asked Sam.

I replied "You may want them to add to your herd. We picked them up on the way from a stallion a few days back."

"OK, Ronnie what do you want for them?"

"How about you give me ten dollars each and the first colts, you can keep all of the fillies."

Sam told me we had a deal. We can cut them out now and move them back to the ranch when we go back for dinner.

Dinner was a fun time for us all, but after a bit, we had to head back to our wagon to get ready to move out in the morning heading for my ranch. Before we left, Beth gave us food to take with us. In the morning we pushed the stock out of the box canyon and headed on north to my home range. I told Juanita how to get by some of the bad spots because this trail had not seen many wagons. The only wagon that had ever come this way was Pa's, and that was when he had gone to town, which was very seldom - at best.

The next two days moved by fast and we had made good time. The closer to the dugout we got I found myself getting more nervous. I still had bad dreams about Pa getting killed, as well as me killing the Indian who had killed him. It was dusk when we pulled in to the dugout. Juanita stayed there while Juan, Tony and I pushed the cattle up into the canyons.

When we got back after an hour or so, Juanita had some coal oil lanterns set out. She also had a fire in the old stove and was cooking dinner. It smelled delicious.

In the morning I saddled up and made a quick run up to see the cattle and then see about finding an elk or deer for camp meat. I hoped to spot an elk getting his last drink before heading back up the hill to lay down and rest in the shade.

Luck was with me. After ground-tying Diamond, I slipped up behind a finger that ran out into the canyon. Slipping over the top, keeping low and behind the trees, I slid in between two pines to take a look at the stream. Standing there, in front of me, was a nice three prong bull elk taking a drink. I waited until he lowered his head to water. And then, the Henry slammed and the elk was down. After I cleaned and loaded it on Diamond, I headed back to camp. Since the weather was not cold enough to leave the meat hanging, we smoked some of the meat, and salted the rest for use later.

For dinner, Juanita cut up the neck for elk stew. I don't know how she can make a meal taste so good. After eating, I told them we needed to talk. For a minute or two, they all had a look, like, "What did I do?"

That's when I just spit the words out. "This is our ranch, not just mine," I told them. "I want you to operate it like it is your ranch, and in fact, it is part yours. But first there is something I want to say, so it is up to you to build what you want and how you want it. Pick a spot you like and build your cabin. I am going to join the Pony Express and ride for them for a while."

Of course the comment made them all look at each other with amazement. I smiled. "It's going to take a few years to build up the herd, and I won't be here if I'm riding for the Pony Express."

"What gave you that idea," Juan said.

"I again saw a poster in Mr. Brown's store. The Pony Express is looking for young men to ride for them, and I'm the right age for it." To their relief, I also told them that Bill Brown would provide the supplies. "He will keep a record for me to pay later when I see him."

I have never seen two people with bigger smiles than Juan and Juanita. Juan was almost speechless, but he did say, "I'm just very glad to have a job."

"Well then, you should be real glad to be part owners of a cattle ranch," I said.

The next day, I put on my old duds and boots. My hat was about out of life, also, but I wanted to look the part. When I rode back to town, Juan went with me. I wanted Diamond to stay with the mares, to keep them safe. I told Juan, "I'm taking Dandy and you can bring him back, if I get the job. When I went in to talk to Mr. Russell who was one of the founders of the Pony Express, Juan stayed outside, waiting to see what would happen next.

Poem by Ron Bell

Hoof beats sounding, By Ron Bell Silver Springs Nevada

Hoof beats sounding

Waiting for the mail on the old pony express trail

Hoof beats sounding, horses talking, the smell of sweat in the air

The Mochila is passed, an impatient stomp of the hoof, stirrups filled

Hoof beats sounding, another rider down the trail

Its getting dark on the trail, the click of rocks on the shoes, looking hard to pick the path

Hoof beats sounding, pushing hard so not to fail

The exchange is coming, in dark of night, the next rider is waiting

Hoof beats sounding, stars are shining, no moon in sight

My time is near, I hear the slap of hoof on the dirt, down the hill around the curve

Hoof beats sounding, Mochila passed, I am up, the bit turned loose, into the night I ride

My time is here, I do my part, the mail moves forward, the night is dark, no light is sight

Hoof beats sounding, down the hill, into the dry wash, hoofs sliding in the sand,

The dark is all around me, out of the wash, my horse smells a friend, the Mochila is passed again.

Hoof beats sounding, off into the night, hoof beats sounding

Chapter 10 DELIVERING HORSES TO CARSON CITY

It was as if the poster was speaking to me. "The Pony Express is looking for young men – orphans, small in stature and able to ride anything with a saddle on its back."

Of course, this had to be me – beat-down hat, holes in my homespun pants, and one shirt to my name - not even taking into account the old pair of rundown boots. What a sight I was, walking in there to say I was their man. Hell, I was only sixteen years old, and it was possible they might not believe me, when I told them I was eighteen and just off the ranch. My thinking was – if they need riders, they will take the word of just about anybody but my heart almost went to the floor when Mr. Russell said, "We need riders - not stable boys."

To which I fired back, "I can ride anything you can find to put under me."

He replied, "Don't get your back up. I was just funning you, boy. By the way what is your handle?"

"Ronnie Campbell." I said

"Well now . . . just sit down and have a little drink of rye to calm your nerves a mite." Wanting to look the part, I took a slug and just about choked to death. After a few pats on the back, I got my breath back. I had to stand there, quiet, while Mr. Russell made a few digs at my lack of drinking ability. He joked that if I rode as bad as my drinking ability, it was clear I would not last the first day. But then to my surprise, he said, "Get your kit," and he gave me directions to the bunk house, saying, "Tell the cook that I said to feed you."

To look genuine, I acted like the best part of getting the job was being able to get the food. "Food's been scarce, after I walked off the ranch," I said. And to anyone who looked at me, they would guess, that all I owned was what they could see. Little would they know that I, actually, was a sixteen year old ranch owner with a sack full of gold nuggets!

When I left the building, I told Juan, "I got the job. You can take Dandy back to the ranch". He had been waiting for me, out of sight, around the corner. Then I went to the bunkhouse as directed.

That night I slept lightly, as I was eager to get started the next day. The sun was just starting to come up when I was shook out and was told to go grab some chuck. I piled in all I could eat, and when I started to slow down, Cookie told me to head to the office. "Report in and pick up your station assignment."

As I was walking to the office, I got a look at five of the best horses I had ever seen - other than Diamond. Man, it looked like they could run! The gray gelding was saddled up. The other four only had halters and lead ropes. My assignment took only a few seconds, and it was this, "Ronnie, we need this string of horses in the Carson City Station. Tie off these four horses and go pick up the packhorse. It's down at the general store, and the packs are loaded with everything you will need. You'll be heading west about 250 miles to your first station. And all six horses are to be delivered to Bolivar Roberts in Carson City as soon as you can get them there. He needs 'em because the Indians took some of his stock. If I was you, I'd be riding all of them. That way you can get to know them. When you do get there, you will be riding for Mr. Roberts until you are told otherwise. That's if you can get the job done. If you can't, get ready to walk home. It's only 250 miles. Here is the map, with your destination marked. It should take you about five days at the most. Get going."

Okay, so the directions took more than a few seconds, but now I knew what I had to do, and by golly, I was going to do it. As the sun came up on my back, I finished tying my pony string to the packhorse. After examining the horses, I decided to name the big gray, "Lighting", because he looked fast.

I just got my leg in the stirrup, when he went straight up and landed hard on all four legs hard. How I stayed in the saddle, I never knew, but with some luck - I was able to pull his head around into my leg. We went around and around for a bit. After the fun was over, I looked up and there was Mr. Russell, standing on the porch with a big smile on his face. "Well son," he said. "That horse is one of the gentle ones. Have fun on your little trip."

*

After I tied the packhorse to the saddlehorn, I was on my way, down the street leading the other five horses. Lighting did give me a few more tests before we decided we liked each other. At my noon break, I found a small stream, leading out of a draw. Here, I worked upstream to find some shade and a spot to take a break. The grass was good along the banks, so I picketed the horses and tested out the coffee pot, I opened up a package and chewed on some hard tack while the horses drank from the stream and grazed for a bit.

After eating, I traded Lighting for the blood bay named Buster. He was a real looker, with a blazed face and two white stockings – and a wise guy too. When I put the saddle blanket on his back and reached down to pick up the saddle, he reached around and pulled the blanket off with his teeth. After playing this game for a bit, I finally picked up the blanket and saddle and put them on him at the same time.

Now for the test – with one foot in the stirrup, I put my other leg over and found the other stirrup. All was well as I gave him a little try, to see if he had any other games he wanted to play. This guy had only two speeds, either he walked - or ran, flat out - and man could he run. After letting him have his way for a mile or so, I took control and headed him back to load up my kit, pick up the other horses, and start the next twenty-five miles.

It took almost that many miles to get this guy to slow down to a trot and soft canter. With the other horses tied to the saddle horn, it did help. After awhile, his walk, trot, and canter was much better. Maybe he was raced at one time or another. If not, he should have been. For one thing, I learned he could outrun all of the rest of the horses, hands down, except Lighting. It's good to know what your horses can and cannot do.

By the time I was ready to find a spot to bed down at the end of the day, I had passed a couple of relay stations. I just kept going. I wanted to reach one of the home stations where there would be food and a stable to put up the horses for the night. During the day I passed a rider who was going east at a full gallop. He was eating a biscuit and we didn't speak. Later at a relay station, I was told he was Larry McPherson.

Dusk was settling in when I saw smoke. It would be full on dark when I reached the Robert's Creek Station, and I pushing hard to get there. When I got close and approached the cabin, I called out to the station manager, who walked out with a rifle in his hands. He looked relieved when he saw me. I introduced myself as a new rider, Ronnie Campbell, and told him I was bringing horses to Bolivar Richards at the Carson City headquarters.

"I am Bill Hartwell," he said.

"Pleased to meet you, I said. Then after getting the horses settled in, I asked him, "What's on the stove?"

"I'm not much of a cook," he said, "But there is some venison stew and rice. That was all he had, as McPherson had taken the last of the biscuit's when he headed east.

"Anything will do me," I told him, and after eating, we sat and talked in front of the big rock fireplace.

Bill told me that there had been some Indian trouble during the past few weeks. "I hope it goes away soon," he said. "For now, I sleep with one eye open."

"Do you switch eyes each night?" I asked, funning with him. He laughed, but I could see it probably was not funny. "Why are the Indians so mad?" I asked.

"Some Pah Utes have been killed by settlers who took Indian land." He said. "And also, some of the women were raped and killed by the same settlers. Then things got worse. Three company men were shot at the Dry Creek station. One of 'em was shot inside the station. Two others died in a running gunfight as they headed to town. It had something to do with Indian women living at the station. That's when Chief Winnemucca started raiding over a large area along the Pony Express trail. His warriors discovered Pony Express stations are a good place to steal horses. That's why we are being hit by raiding parties now."

After hearing that, I also slept with one eye open. In the morning Bill was up and fixed breakfast while I gathered the horses and loaded my packs with supplies.

Before leaving, I told Bill, "To be on the safe side, what stations should I stop at between here and Carson City?"

"Smith's Creek would be about right, but you're gonna have to ride hard to get there before night comes."

"What should I watch for before I get there?" I asked.

"When you leave here, you will drop down into the valley. Grubb Wells will be your first water hole, then on to Dry Creek Station, which is at the bottom of a steep climb. Change horses there cuz you'll be ridin' hard - you'll need to change mounts every hour, to keep the horses fresh.

With an "adios" I was on my way. At Dry Creek Station, I changed horses for the climb over the mountain heading on to Smith Creek Station. I changed mounts many more times. Around noon, I noticed dust rising over the horizon behind me. I didn't think much about it, as there was a little wind. I reached Jacob's Spring Station by mid afternoon and was able to get food for me and grain for my horses. They had had only a little water and grass all day. After giving them a quart of grain each, I headed on to Dry Wells Station. When I passed it, I knew I was about twelve miles from Smith's Station, where I hoped to spend the night and let the horses rest with plenty of hay and grain. That's when I spotted even more dust, off to my left about a half mile behind me. I could see it was closing in on me, so I knew it had to be Indians. Getting close to Smith's Creek Station, I pulled my Henry out of the scabbard and levered a round into the chamber, carrying it as I rode. Pushing my horses into a gallop, we were moving fast to keep the Indians at a safe distance behind me.

This is my friend Sandy Blair and I at Fort Churchill State Park. Sandy Blair is the one who asked me to expand the prologue into this book. Good or bad, thanks Sandy. Yes, the horse is Dandy. Yes my wife Susie was at this photo shoot!!!!!

Photo by Sarah Morey

Chapter 11 RONNIE MEETS A GIRL

I came into Smiths Creek Station at a full gallop looking for some help. A couple of miles back I had been shot at and had some Indians on my tail. I think they wanted my horses. But when I got close to the station the Indians backed off and didn't attack. Bad trouble was coming on with the Indians. Bob Haslam, another Express rider, had told the station master some of the stations had been burned and no horses were left. The Indians had taken all they could get. Bob had just headed back to Carson City just a few hours ago. I knew now for sure I had to get these horses to Carson City and fast.

I told the Station Master I would head out when the moon came up. I would stand a better chance by riding by night. I got the Station Master to draw a map of the trail leading to Carson City along with any watering holes not directly along the trail.

When night settled in I headed out with the map and an idea of land marks to watch for along the trail. The plan was to ride until first light and then find a hiding place off the trail so I could sleep during the day. My pace was fast, and I only walked about 10 minutes each hour. The rest of the time was an extended, ground covering trot with some canter mixed in. By switching between Lighting and Buster every two hours I kept the horses fresh and ready to run if I got jumped. I knew they could outrun any other horse in Nevada.

Seeing the light starting to show in the east, I started looking for a spot to hole up for the day. With a little light, I could see the tracks left by Bob Haslam, heading west with the mail. The tracks showed he was going at a soft trot and not pushing his horse too hard. He knew he had a long way to go with only one horse. If I had only been just a few hours earlier getting into Smith Station, we could have rode west together.

At Cold Springs Station I watered the horses and found a bit of grain that the Indians had not found. I gave that to Buster and Lighting they would need it the most. My horses would need to graze on bunch grass today. I pushed on and found a draw leading away from the trail, so I headed up and got lucky, there was some grass but no water. I unsaddled and got the horses on picket pins so they could graze while I caught a nap in the shade under a bush. I heard Lighting snort and I came wide awake.

Pulling out the Henry, I eased down the draw. When I got close to the trail I could see dust in the air and the tracks of about 20 unshod horses. This was not good, but it was better than having them behind me. I felt that Bob had enough lead to be out of trouble, but they had followed his trail as far as I could see. It was a good thing Lighting had only snorted or I could have been in a real bad spot. It was a good thing that Buster had not smelled them, he is a talker.

I got little rest between moving the horses on to new feed and slipping back out to the edge of the draw and watching. It was a good thing I had taken the time to use some brush to wipe out my tracks leading into the draw. I remembered what Pa would say, "take the extra time." I waited until the sun had dropped and dark had settled in before going back out to the trail. When I got to the opening of the draw I sat a bit, letting the night come to me. Seeing no fires either direction, I moved out with the horses, heading west into the unknown.

From what I had been told, all of the stations between here and Buckland Station were burnt down! The map said the next sure water was at West Gate Station. The problem was that West Gate Station was another thirty miles. My map also told me that about ten miles from my location was little seep, but you could not depend on it having water year around. It was called Sometimes Spring. Tonight I would need to take it slow. The horses needed water, my canteen was out, I had used it on Buster and Lighting - they are my lifeline to escaping the Indians.

I decided to take a chance on the spring. Pushing on into the night, the moon was just now coming up behind me. If the map was right I should be coming up to the canyon anytime. Things sure look different at night. The marker was a bald face rock with a small tree to its right. Could I see it with this light? I would just have to hope.

I had about given up on finding it when, on my right, I could see what looked like the flat rock with a pine on its right. I felt sure I had found what I was looking for, and started into the canyon to have a look see. Moving into the canyon, I hoped I could see hoof prints that would tell me if the Indians had turned off the trail heading for the same spring. Now the bigger question was - Did the Indians camp or just water their horses and move on?

I would need to go in slow. I decided to tie the horses to some brush and slip up with just one horse. I had picked a mare that looked like she could run. I had not ridden her yet, but I had watched her and felt she could run if I needed her to. I got the feeling she had been with a wild herd some time in her past.

This could work to my advantage, she would smell both Indians and water when the others horses might not. With only one horse I could hear better and have a better chance to get away if I needed to make a run for it at night. Moving the horses into some brush just inside of a small finger coming into the canyon, I tied them off and set out to see if we could get to water.

If the Indians had stopped to camp they would have a fire that I could see or smell. That was what I hoped anyway. Working forward at a walk, we stopped from time to time to smell the air and listen for a bit to the night sounds. Hearing no sounds but a few bugs, my hopes were getting higher.

I figured I must be getting close because her ears moved forward and she wanted to pick up the pace. I had to check her back and take it easy as we worked our way forward. I would have walked on past if she had not turned into some brush and found the spring. We seemed to be alone. The water was just refilling after the Indians had watered their horses, but it would be enough for my horses.

I let her have a drink, she had earned it. Turning back down the trail, I picked up the other horses. After refilling my canteens and changing my saddle back to Buster, I headed back out on the trail leading me west to Buckland Station and safety. From what I had been told, Sand Springs Station had bad water but I would see about that in a while.

Light was starting to show when we made Sand Springs Station. The water tank was full and the water was bad tasting. After a little coaxing, the horses got down some water. I watched each drink to make sure they swallowed at least 10 swallows. We still had a lot of ground to cover. After they all drank what I felt they would need, I headed around the south end of the dry lake bed.

This part of the trail was going to be a hard ride. I would be riding along the base of the mountains leading to a low pass. That would take me into some low ground and dry lake beds leading me to the Carson Sink and Hooten Wells.

When I got around the dry lake, I started dropping into and out of some steep dry-washes cutting across the trail. I then climbed over a small pass between a couple of hills and dropped into the Carson Sink. I was in open country now with no way to hide. Keeping my eyes open would keep me alive. I was watching for any movement, but it was most important to watch my horses. Buster would be the one to get me into trouble because he liked to make noise. Buster may be noisy, but the Indian ponies would never catch him if we had to run for it.

I was watching out for Indians from any direction now. I had moved off the trail to keep my dust low. I kept watch for other dust along my path and, seeing none, I moved on, hoping to reach Buckland Station by nightfall. Changing horses every two hours was now helping me a great deal. We had made good time and the horses seemed fresh enough if I needed to make a hard run into Buckland Station.

When I reached Hooten Wells, it was also burned down, but the water tank was full. After watering the horses, I headed out west hoping to make the last run to Buckland without any trouble. It was getting late in the day when I made out the trees around Buckland Station and along the Carson River. Easing the horses into a trot, I knew I would have a hot meal and a sweet hay loft to sleep in.

When I came into the station everybody came out to see who I was and how I got in alive. The Indians had been raising hell all along the trail. Many outlying ranches had been burned and people killed. With some help I got the horses taken care of and headed in to get a meal. I had been short of real food other than beef jerky and hard tack by not being able to have a fire. That also meant I hadn't had any coffee for several days and I wanted some good, hot coffee too.

Everyone was trying to ask questions all at once. I was doing my best to tell them I had just been lucky and made it without any problems. My eyes woke up when a young girl came over to my table to take my order. She was so good looking, I could not get out what I wanted. I just kept looking at her. After a few starts I did get my order in and she had told me her name was Abby. I don't think I had ever heard a nicer name in my life.

I was still being pestered by people asking about my trip. Abby just came over and said "let this man eat, his meal is getting cold." She said: this man. I had never been called a man before. From her it sounded just great. I had never even talked to a girl before and she had just came over and called me a man.

I was red all the way up to the top of my head, my heart was beating fast and my hands were sweating now as bad as when I had had to kill the Indian. Then she came back again with my water and more coffee. I was trying to act normal but I think she could tell I was having trouble sitting still.

When I had finished my food she came back to ask if I would like anything else. I said I would, I would like another cup of coffee. She went to get the coffee pot and when she came back she just sat down and started talking to me. Right off the bat she asked how old I was. I said "well, I told the Pony Express that I was eighteen, but don't tell them, I am only sixteen."

Abby said, "we are the same age then. I thought you looked older by a year or so."

"If it would make you happy I could be eighteen if you like."

"No" she said, "sixteen is just fine with me." After a bit she said she had to go back to work and asked if I would be back in the morning to eat. I told her "not only was that a yes but I think a hell yes."

I was offered a real bed to sleep in that night - man what a change. When the sun was coming up I went out to check on the horses and get ready to head to Carson City after breakfast. When I went in to eat Abby was waiting for me and sat me in the corner out of the way. She got my order and after she set the food down, she sat at my table again.. Oh my, my day was looking up. I was the only one eating then, so Abby sat and we talked. It was a little better today talking to her after the shock of yesterday. She was nice. I found out she had been left alone somewhat like I had been. Her folks had been killed en-route to California and she had been offered a place to stay if she helped with serving meals and helping around the station. Abby said that she had driven their team and wagon alone the last month of the trip. She told me that sometimes one of the older boys came to help but only a few hours at a time.

We talked about the deal she had worked out with Mr. Buckland so she could keep her equipment her Mom and Dad had in the wagon. Mr. Buckland could use her horses if he would feed and take care of them, and she could have them back when she wanted them. Her wagon still had all of the equipment her Dad would have needed to set up their ranch that he had wanted in California.

We both talked about our folks some and what we wanted to do later. I finished eating and said I had to get the horses on to Carson City. I needed to get on my way. After paying, I started out to the corrals and Abby went along with me so we could keep talking.

I had Lighting saddled and the others tied and ready to go. I was having a hard time getting into the saddle and leaving. Abby said, "well, you do have to go but could you come back and see me some time soon. I like talking to you." "Abby," I told her, "I will be back as soon as possible." I was getting red again, I could feel it and she just thought it was funny. I said I hope to get the assignment in this area, but I will come back whenever I can. I like to talk to you too. Turning the horses west, I rode off, heading for Carson City. If I rode hard I could make the 50 miles today.

Chapter 12 FINDING HORSES

After meeting Abby I had planned to come back whenever I could, in fact I may just make a special trip just to get to talk to her. Climbing out of the river bottom leaving Buckland behind, I followed the trail past Fort Churchill, but there was just too much activity for me to bother to go in and look around. I wanted to get into Carson City.

The ride on toward Carson City was without any problems. Midday I arrived at Dayton Station or should say trading post. It had a nice location. The buildings were set back up by some small hills and the river was just across the wagon road from its door. With Dayton falling behind me I should be into Carson with some light left. I was making good time.

Bolivar Roberts was waiting at the gate to the station when I came in at a shuffle foot trot. "Well son, what is your name?" "Ronnie Campbell, I said.

"I got word that some kid made his way through all of the Indian raids and had some replacement horses with him." Bolivar said, "how in hell did you get here in one piece?"

Ronnie said, "If you have a little food and some coffee we could talk about my ride."

Bolivar gave the order to one of the men to take the horses to the stable, get them some grain and give them a little extra hay. In the morning he wanted them checked over real good, and to have the blacksmith check their feet. He wanted them ready to go by noon.

Bolivar turned to Ronnie saying, “This is a trip I need to hear about. Let’s go sit down and have some dinner and talk it over.” During dinner Ronnie talked about getting on Lighting. “He just went straight up and tried to unseat me.” Ronnie told Bolivar about how much fun Mr. Russell got out of seeing the rodeo in front of the general store when he was getting ready to head west.

”The real story started when I got to Smith Creek Station. I knew I was in trouble. I’ve seen Indian trouble first hand, and now I had 190 miles to ride with no support and 5 horses to deliver to you. Can you believe this? Bob Haslam had just started back to Carson City only hours ahead of me. I could have tried to catch him but the station manager, Mr. Trumbo, told me to get some sleep and leave after dark and ride until daylight. Then he said that when the light starts to show, find a spot to lay low during the day.” So then I went on and told Mr. Roberts about how I slipped in behind a raiding party of Indians that was working their way west. I had hoped that they would just keep moving. That is how I made it to Buckland without having any problems.

Roberts said, “I want you to get some sleep and be ready to get on the trail in the morning. I have a problem and you are going to be taking it on.” What’s not to like - bed, food, roof. Life is good today, but what about in the morning. Mr. Roberts had said nothing about what he had in mind. .

The sun was edging over the hills to the east when I rolled out and got dressed. Breakfast was on the table when I sat down in the dining hall at the station. The cook’s helper filled my cup with coffee. Trail food had been lean so with biscuits, bacon, large steak and eggs I was doing my best to clean off the whole table.

After slowing down some I noticed a newspaper from Sacramento on the table. The front page was telling about a random killing of a young Mexican and his palomino stud being stolen. The owner of the horse was Victor Morales and was the youngest son of Don Jose Morales. His rancho was one of the largest ranchos around Sacramento. They raise some of the best Palominos in California. Sheriff Johnson in Sacramento had a feeling the killer was a man called Jon Dugan, the markings on the horse matched two other local killings. Looking up from the paper, I saw Mr. Roberts walk in with a big smile on his face. I knew I was in trouble for sure.

"Well, son, I have a job for you. Having just ridden along the trail I need to know what you found at the stations along the way." Finding ink, pen and paper he started to make a list of the conditions of the stations I had passed. "I am sending a crew out to repair the damage and you are going to help me re-stock each station with horses. Today we will go out and take a look at some replacement horses from some of the local ranches."

Ronnie told Bolivar he could get 10 real fine horses from a ranch out east in the Ruby's if he wanted them. "We could re-stock all of the stations from the east heading this way. I could ride out and purchase the 10 from Sam Applegate, if that is what you want."

Bolivar said, "Well, let's just see what kind of horses we find in the next few days." Over the next two days, I told him about all of the stations along the way. Later in the day Bob Haslam and Andy Sams added some more information about what they had seen.

Bolivar Roberts took notes every day from other riders as they came through the station. On the third day he said, "saddle up and we will go out and take stock of what horses we can find." During our ride we found out that most ranches had pulled in their ranch hands and prepared for a fight with the Indians, if need be. At the Flying T Ranch, the owner, Mr. Birdwell, said he would sell some of his horses, but asked Bolivar why he would take any color now, when the last time he would only take grays.

Mr. Roberts said the Indians now have about all of the grays that had been purchased back in the spring of 1860. I think I could get along with just good horses this time around. Mr. Birdwell asked how many horses would be needed to get back in operation. "Look, Ronnie, you have 6 good mounts that you brought with you." Bolivar said, "are they all good stock and can they run?" Ronnie said; "Lighting and Buster are the best but the other four are sound, and they can run, but they can't keep up with Lighting or Buster." "Ok" Bolivar said "I need twenty that can run." He asked Birdwell "how much do you want for the twenty horses?" "Well", Mr. Birdwell said, "how about $100.00 each." "Damn" Bolivar said, "I can't pay that kind of money, you got to do better than that." Birdwell came back with, "you do know horses are in short supply due to the Indian raids." Bolivar said, "I think I will take a look around some and get back to you later in the week." Turning to Ronnie he asked "what about the ten horses you told me about?"

"Look, Mr. Roberts, I trained all of them and they are all great horses. The stallion is a Standard Bred, the mares are Mustangs. They all stand 15 hands to 15-2 and like I said, they can run."

Bolivar said "How long would it take you to get them to Spring Creek Station? Maybe you could meet the relay station rebuilding crews when they get there or soon after. What do you think? Look, Ronnie, could you make the trip in a couple of weeks if you got started in a day or two? What do you think about that plan?"

"I need to pay the owner $60.00 a head for these horses," Ronnie said. "That should be a good price. He is kind of back in the hills and would be glad to have the cash, I am sure."

Bolivar said, "With the price of horses around Carson City that would work for me. Are you sure you can slip past the Pah Ute's again. They have killed a lot of men and made off with a lot of good horses over the last few weeks."

Ronnie said, "Well, Mr. Roberts, how about I take Lighting and Buster? That way I can keep them fresh and will be able to outrun any horse in Nevada." Bolivar agreed and wanted to get back to the station to lay out the trip. He could have the repairs made to the five stations while I was getting the horses.

During dinner they set it up that Ronnie would head out in the morning with the two horses, both saddled and ready to ride. This way he would not need to stop to change tack on the trip. Ronnie loaded two saddle bags, one on each horse with extra shells for his rifle and food to last the trip on each horse. On each horse he also had a Navy Colt plus two extra cylinders for each of the pistols. The pistols and extra cylinders were in holsters in front of each saddle. Ronnie said: "Mr. Roberts, I hope you don't mind if I keep my Henry with me, I feel lost without it in my hand. Look, Mr. Roberts, I am going to Buckland Station today and lay low until dark tomorrow, then I will get on the trail heading east. I would rather slip out after dark just in case anyone is watching the coming and going. We will have no moon so I should be able to get away clean.

Chapter 13 RIDING BACK TO THE RUBY'S

The hills to the east were just showing light when I eased out of the stable heading east toward Buckland Station. I pushed hard changing horses from time to time along the way. Lighting and Buster could cover ground by loping for fifteen to twenty minutes and trotting for thirty minutes, I only dropped to a walk a couple of times to let them get their breath. But at all times I had the Henry ready for action.

I pulled into Buckland in time for a late dinner. Abby had a smile for me when I came in and sat down to eat. "Well, you did come back. Is it to see me or other reasons?"

I said, "Mr. Roberts is sending me back down the trail to pick up some other horses on the west side of the Ruby Mountains."

Abby said, "Oh no, you can't do that. The Indians are still raiding along the trail. We are hearing reports every day."

"Look," I said, "I made it through last time and I can do it again, I have two of the fastest horses in Nevada and I am well armed."

I put my order in for steak and all of the trimmings. Mr. Roberts had given me some money to pay for food and the horses I would buy from Sam Applegate. After a short wait, I had a large steak with everything on it, my coffee cup was filled, I was doing just fine. Abby asked me when do I ride east.

I answered "after dark tomorrow night. I am going to bunk in the stable tonight and I will be around all day tomorrow. If you want to visit I can meet you out by the stable." I was sitting on a box by the corral talking to Buster and Lighting when Abby walked up. After talking a bit, Abby said she had to get back. "Will I see you in the morning?" Ronnie went to sleep with Abby on his mind.

After breakfast I went about checking my gear, taking a good look at the two horses I would depend on for this ride. Abby dropped by the stable about mid-morning to say hi. I walked back to get some lunch with her. After eating I said, "I think I am just to go down along the bank of the river and take a nap this afternoon."

Abby said, "Well I may just come down and sit with you for a while, I have time off until dinner time." Ronnie headed out toward the river hoping Abby would show up to talk some.

I had dropped off to sleep in the shade of the cottonwoods, listening to the birds chirping. When I woke up I had company. Abby was just sitting there watching me sleep. I woke up with a start. I had not heard her slip up and sit down. "Abby you about scared the life out of me, I had expected to hear you walk up - if you came at all. "

Abby said, "do you want me to go back to work or do you want to talk?."

I had never talked to a girl before. This was all new and I felt like I was on fire. "Look Abby, I am new at this talking to a girl stuff. How do I get started? Can I ask you about your folks, or is it too hard to talk about that this soon?"

Abby said, "it is hard to talk about it, but you also had the same thing happen, so I think it will be easer to talk to you."

Abby asked me to tell her about my ranch. I told her "I kind of have a small ranch back in the hills east of here and I have a man and his wife working it until I get back. I like to ride fast horses and riding for the Pony Express looked like fun to me."

Abby said, "well, Ronnie we do have a lot to talk about. Just how big is your ranch?"

"Abby I don't want anyone to know the location of my ranch at this time, it is not that small. I only have around a hundred and fifty head of young cows with ten bulls. By next year I should have about twice that many cattle. I would like to ride the Pony Express for a year. But look, I want to know a little more about you and how you got to Buckland. Let's save my ranch details until later. Would that be ok?"

Abby said, "I am from Pennsylvania. My mom and dad planned to start a ranch in California but they never made it, but you know that already."

Ronnie asked, "what will you do now that they are gone?"

She said, "well, I don't know yet but time will tell me what to do. I still have all of their ranch supplies and I could go on over to California if I choose, but I like it around here for now." Then she smiled and said "I like to talk to you. You just need to keep coming back to see me."

"I am going back to the station now so you can catch some shut eye. Do be careful, if you get hurt I won't have anyone to talk to. Everyone is older, or too forward to suit me." Abby reached down and touched Ronnie's hand and said to please come back and then walked away with a swish of her skirt.

Did this really happen or was I dreaming? But when I looked toward Buckland, Abby was just walking around the corner of the building. I knew at that time I would never get back to sleep so I just laid there watching the clouds pass over through the trees and listening to the rustle of the leaves. What a day!

The sun was setting when I got up and walked to the barn to saddle the horses and get ready for my ride into danger. I could feel the tension building, but I knew it would be ok once I got on the trail.

The cloud cover would help with my slipping away without being seen. When it was full dark I heard someone coming to the corral. With the soft step and the swish of a skirt I knew it was Abby, "Abby, over here," I said.

"Ronnie I just had to come out to wish you a safe trip." She walked up, she laid her hand on my arm, then looked up and smiled at me.

When I stepped up into the saddle she took a step forward and touched my hand, pulling it down and laying it on her cheek and said, "be careful."

Turning toward the river, I chose to not use the bridge. I just eased down stream and walked across the river then up the bank on the far side. Just a little further past the trees I picked up the trail heading east. I decided to trot most of the night, changing horses each hour to keep them fresh. When you had Lighting or Buster in an extended trot they could cover ground.

I was about at Hooten Wells when I slowed down to a walk. I could just make out the burned out station. Buster had his ears forward. I think he was picking up my feelings. The Henry was ready. I pulled up and listened - trying to hear any movement. Neither horse seemed to hear any noises. Taking a few steps forward I stopped again to listen. Then I moved on in to let the horses get a drink. I wanted to know how much water they drank so I kept my hand on the throat strap and counted 14 before Lightning finished and I did the same with Buster. That should last them to the next water.

I was well on my way to what was left of the Carson Sink Station when I smelled smoke. I had that scary feeling climbing up the back of my neck and in my gut. Someone was at the Carson Sink Station and it could only be Indians.

This was going to be a problem. Stopping back about a half mile from the station, I turned south into a small draw. I would need to make a wide swing around the station in hope to get past the Indians without anyone seeing or hearing me. The sand is soft so they should not hear me when I passed to the south and then east to swing back onto the trail.

The next problem was I needed to keep Buster from talking to the Indian ponies. Walking slowly and talking softly to Lighting and Buster, trying to keep them quiet, I was about back to the trail when Buster smelled them and whinnied. I mounted Buster and off we went out at a canter for a mile, then down to a ground eating trot.

I wanted to save them if I needed some real speed later. It was hard to see the trail so I let Buster pick his way. I had a good lead but I wanted them to push their horses to catch up with me. Then I would run their tired horses into the ground.

Both Lighting and Buster had been on grain and good hay for some time, so I felt the Indian ponies could never catch me in a long hard run. It was hard to keep at a slower pace when I wanted to let them have their heads. We cantered again for a while. Then I jumped onto Lighting so Buster could get some rest.

It was still dark enough that I could not see the Indians coming up behind me but I started to hear them. They knew they had gained on me and had been pushing their horses hard. I kept looking back over my shoulder to get a look: I could see them now and they were getting closer. It was about time to let Buster and Lighting make their run.

I was thinking back on my first trip to Carson City. The trail would come out of Carson Sink into a little draw leading me over a small rise, then the sand hill. I figured I would lose the Indians there.

I came over the hill and the horses had to slide most of the way down to the bottom. Then the trail followed along the base of the hills, skirting the dry lake bed to Sand Springs. I dropped the reins on Lighting and off we went flat out, when I came to the draw. I slowed down a little to make sure he could see and keep on the trail.

The Indians had started to lose ground so I jumped back onto Buster. We had to climb up the sand hill and Buster was strong. Slowing to a trot, we headed up the hill. I could still hear the Indians but they had lost ground. Buster was blowing hard when we reached the top but he was still game. Changing back to Lighting we were over the top and skirting along the broken hills leading to Sand Springs Station.

Slowing down to a walk, I gave my horses a rest. When the Indians came to the climb leading up the sand hill they pulled up and went back to their camp. They had to know they could never catch me after that climb. I kept the horses at a walk for about thirty minutes, letting them catch their breath. Man, that was a ride and I was sure glad I picked these two horses for this trip. I knew they could outrun about anything the Indians had.

Sand Springs should be just a few miles ahead so I picked back up to a trot and started covering ground. Getting close to Sand Springs, I could see some light starting to show to the east. The water was bad there but the horses got a little and I started on to Cold Springs Station and better water.

Heading up and over the pass, it was getting light now. I needed to find a spot to hole up and watch my back trail for dust. I was hoping I would be alone on into Cold Springs. The horses could use some rest so I worked my way into a little draw off to the north side of the trail, finding a good spot to stop for the day. I went back and brushed out my tracks leading into my location.

I loosened the cinches and tied the horses to some brush. I walked back along a game trail leading to a little bench, so I could overlook my back trail. My rifle was ready if needed, but I felt I was alone and hoped that the Indians that gave chase went back and would leave me alone.

I found a large boulder to lean back on and sat down to rest. I pulled some jerky from the saddle bags and started to eat. My water from the canteen tasted good and helped to wash down the jerky. The sun was hot but by moving a few times during the day I was able to get a few short naps in the shade of the boulder.

The sun was starting to go down. I had been checking my back trail every hour or so. I slipped back down and pulled the cinch tight on both horses and moved out slow. The ground started to drop some as I made it around the edge of the hill.

This part of the country was open with washes cutting across the trail. Without the clouds I could see quite well with just a sliver of a moon and stars. I kept the horses at a fast trot with some walking most of the night.

I stopped one time to let both horses rest for an hour so they could get a little grass in them. Morning was coming to the hills to the east and starting to show some light. I found a wash with a little cover leading off the trail. I would rest the horses for a while, then I would ride during the day today.

I was hoping to get past the Indians as soon as I could. Heading east, with the sun in my face, I decided to go slowly, not wanting to ride into trouble and not being able to see it coming. The rest had helped both horses but I had worked them hard and wanted to keep them as fresh as I could. I was hopeful not to have another hard run until they had time to get some real rest and good feed.

The sun was getting high, so I started looking for a spot with some good grass and that would have a good view of my back trail. I hoped to get the horses an hour rest if I could. They had earned it. After sitting down and watching for a bit, I noticed some dust rising a long ways back but it looked like it was heading my way.

Not being one to take a chance, I felt it better to pull up the cinches and, using my hat, I gave them both a little drink. Using my bandana, I wet it and washed out their nostrils before hitting the trail. My best guess it was about four hours into Cold Springs Station.

Stepping up onto Lighting, we headed east at a ground eating trot. I held them in a little to save energy in case I needed to make a run for it. My best guess was I had about an hour lead on the Indians coming up from behind. I wanted who was on my tail to think they could catch me because they were gaining on me fast.

Like the last run we had, I wanted them to think they had me and would push their horses to the limit. Lighting and Buster could cover a lot of ground fast if need be. After about one hour I changed over to Buster and picked it up a little. By the way they were gaining on me I would need to be ready to show them some real dust in about another thirty minutes. I think they were riding some of the stolen Pony Express horses they took during the raids.

I was now only about a mile ahead of them and they were making a run at me. When they got closer I could see that at least two of the lead horses were grays. Damn - they did have better horses. Now I felt I might be in trouble. Bolivar had purchased a lot of grays early last year and they could also run.

Buster could hear them coming and I could feel him wanting me to let him go. I am talking to Buster and Lighting "easy boy, easy boy, not yet boy." When the first rifle shot came close I turned them loose and we lit out like we were on fire. I let them run hard for about fifteen minutes then I changed horses again. We were running flat out. Having not heard any more shots for a while, I pulled back to a trot and turned to take a look. The Indians had turned back and were walking back to the west.

We walked east toward Cold Springs Station feeling a lot better. This is where if I had problem it could get bad. My horses had two hard runs on them and I had no way to know if there were any Indians already at Cold Springs Station. Buster and Lighting needed some water, food and rest. Would they get it?

I was betting on the raids all being west of Cold Springs Station. My plan was when I got close to the station, I would slip up to the north about a half mile off the trail and sit a bit and see if I had any company waiting on me.

I saw Cold Springs Station off in the distance so I eased off the trail and skirted the station to the north. I had to ease around to the east of the station so I would have the wind in my face. I had to worry because Buster liked to talk, when ever he smelled another horse. He had gotten me in trouble back at Hooten Wells, so I was keeping my eye on him. I was riding Lighting so I might be able to get my hand over Buster's nose if he tried to whinny. Working my way around until the wind was in my face, picking up no smell or sound, the horses seemed to be ok.

I was watching their ears to see if they picked up any noise I could not hear. I was downwind from the station now, walking in slow, taking a few steps then stopping and listening. I had the Henry ready if anything moved, but it looked like I was in luck.

Easing up to the watering trough, I stepped down and got a drink then refilled my canteens. taking a look around to see what was left of the Cold Springs Station. What the fire hadn't destroyed the Indians had.

Going back the way I came so the tracks would be in only one area, I stopped and got some brush and removed the tracks the best I could. Getting back aboard, I moved off to the east and then south for about a mile before picking up the trail east to Smith Creek Station

This part of the trail was real flat to look at but is broken up with washes cutting across it. Hoping I could find a spot to watch my back trail and let the horses rest some and eat for a while, I found a draw coming in from the north cutting the trail on its way to the south. This held some promise. Turning off the trail to the north I found some good grass. With the horses grazing, I climbed the bank of the draw to keep watch and chewed on some jerky. After an hour or so, the horses had a belly full of grass. Easing back down the draw to the trail I headed off toward the hills that held the Smith's Creek Station and, I hope, for some food and rest for me and the horses.

Chapter 14 PUSHING ON TO SAM'S RANCH

It was late afternoon when I rode into Smith Creek Station at a trot, with no holes in me or the horses. Mr. Trumbo said, "you must not have learned much on your last trip. Now you are doing it again." Then he asked me if I was nuts, making this ride alone. Well, I spoke right up saying. "When you have the two of the fastest horses in Nevada it sure helps, but yes I could also be nuts." Trumbo had a reputation of being a bad ass and best to be left alone. He had shot a rider named Montgomery Maze in the hip a short while ago.

After stripping the gear off the horses, both got a good rubdown and some grain. Making sure their shoes were ok, I turned them out into the corral to roll and get some hay and water. I would come out later and give each another small bucket of grain. That would help them recover from being pushed so hard.

I walked into the station and asked when dinner would be ready and do you have a bed?

Trumbo said, "you can have the hay mow if you want."

I was done in and needed sleep. During dinner we talked about the Pah Ute raids. I asked if he had any news of Indian problems heading east. Mr. Trumbo said that he had not had any problems yet and hoped to keep it that way.

During dinner I told him about having to outrun the Indians on two different times on my way east and I was pleased with the outcome. After dinner I went out to check on the horses and find a good spot in the hay loft to sleep. Rolling out my tarp on the hay, I lay down and called it a night. Morning would be here soon enough.

The sun was filtering in through the cracks in the boards when I rolled out to get a bite to eat. With a plate full of antelope steak and eggs and homemade bread, I was in heaven. Trumbo and I must have finished off the whole pot of coffee.

I asked if I could use one of his horses for a little bit, I wanted to ride back a few miles and take a swing around to see if the station was being watched before I headed on east. I was only gone for an hour or so but found no tracks in the area. Saddling up and loading my supplies back into my saddle bags I was off heading east.

*

With a good meal under my belt I headed east to Dry Wells Station. I didn't slow down until I reached Jacob's Spring Station. Then I let the horses get a drink to get ready to make the climb up and over three small mountains. One climb before Dry Creek would take me to just under 8,000 feet then drop down into Dry Creek Station. I would give the horses a chance to graze along the stream for an hour or so while I got a drink and some food. Grubb Wells would be out on the flat land and then I would make the climb back on top at Roberts Creek Station.

After leaving Roberts Creek I would be climbing up and down some mountains. I would then stop for a short time at Diamond Springs Station where the water was the best along the trail.

Jacob's Well Station would be my last stop before turning north east to get to Jim Brown's store, then another two day ride to get up to Sam Applegate's place.

*

With a little rest and some grain, the horses were ready to travel. After about two hours I found a spot where I could check my back trail. All looked good so we started to cover more ground. I wanted to get to Jim's store to see how much Juan had spent on supplies getting his ranch house built. I should have two hard days ride, but we would make good time.

I was still trading horses every two hours. With the Indians behind me I was ready to have a real meal and a fire. Jerky is okay but I wanted my coffee hot and bacon crisp. I had a good start so I made an early camp, finding a small draw leading off the trail to some rocks and trees. Working my way past the rocks, I found a small seep coming out from the base of the hill, the pool was small, but taking turns, I had enough water for coffee and the horses. The horses had some good grass so with the picket pins in the ground and the fire started I was ready to settle in and enjoy my meal. This would be a good spot to camp on the way back with the horses.

Dinner finished, I picked up the Henry and walked back out to the trail and settled in for a while as the sun was setting and the night closing in. Picking up my saddle and blanket, I walked back a ways behind the fire and rolled up for the night. The two horses were just a few feet away cropping grass. What a great way to go to sleep.

Light was just showing when I woke up. I just laid there watching the horses for a bit to see if they heard any thing. They were making the best of the last grass so I rolled out and picked up my boots and checked for any critters. Finding none, I pulled them on and went to see if I had any coals left in last nights fire.

Picking up some pine needles, I brushed back some ash and found some coals. Dropping the needles and some pine cones on and blowing a little, I had a fire going. I started the coffee and cut up some bacon strips in my frying pan, then pulled out a couple of biscuits to sop up the grease. With breakfast over, I saddled the horses and picked up camp. We would cover some miles today. Dumping the last of the coffee on the fire and kicking dirt over the coals, I was ready to ride.

Then I stepped up and headed east with Lighting and Buster nose to nose at a gallop, I would make Jim Brown's store late today. I would only take a short rest at noon and then push on east. I was on a mission now. Buster and Lighting liked this fast pace. Their ears were forward and they were moving at a trail eating gate. They were really getting in shape now. We had climbed some big hills and they were still picking them up and laying them down.

The sun was just going down when I came in at a trot to the store. Jim was surprised to see me back so soon. "Well son, what are you doing back and riding two horses?"

"Well," I said, "you feed me and we can have a talk about a lot of stuff." Jim knew about the Pah Ute raids back to the west. No one was heading in that direction until the Army had a chance to clean up the Indian problem.

*

We sat and talked about my trip and I told him that I was on my way to Sam's place to buy ten head of his horses for Bolivar Roberts in Carson City. He is in charge of the Pony Express there. Then I was going to take them back with me to restock the Pony Express horses that been stolen in the Indian raids.

He laughed when I told him about tricking the Indians into chasing me so hard that they ran their horses into the ground. We got around to what I owed him. Juan had been in a couple of times getting building supplies but it sounded like he was coming along real fine.

Jim said, "It sure looks like you have a real worker in that Juan. His wife is real nice too, she has asked me if I could sell some the things she makes. "She has a real hand for making baskets and it looks like she has made a kiln to fire clay pots. Take a look and tell me what you think." Jim walked over to a shelf in the store. "I only have one or two left because they sell about as fast as she brings them in."

Ronnie said "I had no idea Juanita could make clay bowls and baskets, what a surprise."

"Look Ronnie, I still have some of the gold you left, so you still don't owe me anything. Juanita is using her stuff I sell to pay for the supplies so your money is lasting longer. Like I said, you have a real find in that family."

"Jim, can I bunk down in the barn and stable the horses for the night, I want to be on my way at first light." I asked.

Jim said, "ok and the cook will have some food ready for you when you are ready to go. Just saddle up and bring the horses around. Breakfast will be ready." The barn had a hay loft and that make a great place to sleep.

I fed the horses and added about a quart of oats for a little extra punch. Then I climbed up to the loft and went to sleep.

The roosters were crowing as the sun was trying to climb over the hills. I got to my feet, shook the hay out of my bedroll, and rolled up my kit. I climbed down the ladder and saddled the horses then walked them around to the front of the store. Both Buster and Lighting were stepping high. I thought the grain was doing a good job. I had better get both feet in the stirrups when I get aboard today.

Breakfast and some coffee down, I walked out to climb aboard and see what Lighting had waiting for me. He just humped up a little for a jump or two but then settled down to his ground eating trot. I had a feeling we would cover some ground today. Buster kept pulling on the lead rope so I dropped the reins and let both horses go. I let them run for about fifteen minutes to get the edge off then I dropped them back to a stiff trot, changing horses about every hour. We were covering ground.

Their trot was like most other horses canter. The thing that got me was how smooth they were at that gate. They must have some Standard Bred blood in them like Diamond. I was looking forward to seeing how Diamond had done with his bunch of mares."

If I had the time I would like to race Buster and Diamond to just see who is the fastest, but that would need to be another time.

The night was closing in when I came to the spot I wanted to camp. It had water and feed for the horses along with protection from the wind. Wind is about an everyday thing in Nevada.

With the horses on picket lines, I fixed dinner. Then I pulled back into the trees to sleep. With my Henry by my side and the two horses keeping watch I would be able to sleep some tonight. When on the trail you never sleep well, you wake at every sound. That is, if you want to stay alive!

Waking in the morning, I got a drink of water and pulled out a biscuit to chew on. I had a mind to get along quickly to Sam's and Beth's ranch. I would chew on some jerky during the day, heading toward the ranch.

I couldn't wait to see Little John and ask him if he had all the wood split. If all went well with Sam. After paying him for the horses, I could ride back to my ranch to check on the progress. The next afternoon, who did I see riding off a ridge but Little John and he was heading my way. He had his Spencer laying across his legs when he galloping up.

"Well damn it's been a day or so from when you left, what's with the two horses Ronnie?"

"I needed to make a fast trip. I need to talk to Sam, so let's pound some saddle leather." Little John turned and put the spurs to his horse, he got a good jump on me. Buster liked to be in the lead, so it took only a short run when we eased up beside Little John. I looked over and smiled. Then, letting Buster have his head, Lighting was running neck and neck with Buster. We left Little John eating our dust.

In a bit I pulled back to a canter and waited for Little John to catch up. He said "those two sure could make a trip a little shorter." We were getting close to the ranch house so we pulled back to a walk to cool out the horses. Sam would not like to see three horses breathing hard and sweating turned out in his corral. By the time we got to the ranch the horses had cooled down enough so Sam would not take any bark off of us.

Sam and Beth came out to see who was coming to the ranch yard. Back in this country you had so little, if any, company. "Hey Ronnie," "what're you doing with two horses? Did you lose someone, or what?"

"Nah, I just had to make some time."

Little John said "these are two of the fastest horses I have ever seen, Pop. They left me like I was stopped."

Ronnie said, "Sam, we need to talk a bit about some, or I should say all, of the three year olds we broke last winter. I need to purchase them for a man over in Carson City, Nevada."

Sam asked "do you have cash money?"

I said yes. "What do you need if I take all ten?"

Sam came back with "I could not take anything less than forty dollars a head.

"Well Sam, we have a deal but, it will be for sixty dollars a head. Would you take that?"

"Damn son, I could take that any day." Sam grinned.

"Ok, get me a bill of sale and have them ready for me to leave in three days. Sam, I need to leave my two horses with you to give them both a rest! I need a couple of horses to ride back to my place. I need to check up on things at my ranch."

Sam and Beth both asked if I could stay the night but I said no, "I need to get there and back in three days. It is still a hard ride." Little John was heading out the door and was back in just a few minutes with two horses and was changing saddles.

"Here is your money from my boss, Bolivar Roberts. I will be back in three days."

Beth said "hold on just a bit. I will get you some meat and bread to take with you." She rolled the food up in an oil cloth and handed it to me, saying "this should cover you on the ride back to your ranch."

Part of the pictures shot by Richard Massey, Sarah Morey and Nick McCabe all local people

Fort Churchill State Park in the background down the road form Silver Springs Nevada

Chapter 15 CHECKING ON THE RANCH

The two horses Sam loaned me were good but far slower than Buster and Lighting. Three days rest and some grain would do my horses a lot of good. My trip back to Smith Creek Station would take longer and not be as hard on Lighting and Buster. Having to handle the extra horses will slow us down some.

Knowing the trail was a great help so I rode late before making camp. It was dark when I got to the little stream I was looking for. Stripping the saddles off and getting the horses on some grass and water I ate some of the meat and bread that Beth had packed for me and went to sleep with my Henry laying in easy reach if needed. I felt sure if anything came close, one or both of the horses would blow or start moving around and wake me.

The hills were just showing gray when I rolled out. Knocking out my boots I discovered a critter in one of them. Pulling on my boots and putting a little cold water on my face, I saddled up and started out for the ranch.

I wouldn't reach the ranch until late, but I would push hard so we would have some time to talk. At noon I stopped long enough to water the horses and let them graze a bit, then back on the trail to the ranch.

The sun was just setting behind the hills with the clouds showing red. Stopping out a bit, I called out to the house to let them know I was there. Juan came out with a rifle but when he saw who it was, he called me in. What a sight it was when I walked my horse into the ranch yard. I could see that the wall was up and part of the roof was on Juan's house.

Juan said, "Ronnie, what are you doing back? We would have never thought to see you this soon."

I said, "Well, I had to come back to buy some horses for the Pony Express in Carson City, the Indians stole about all of their horses."

Juanita came out and said "come in, look how the house is coming along. We are starting to live in the cabin even without the roof."

"Man this place is looking good. Now fill me in on what you are doing and how are Diamond and the mares doing."

"Here Ronnie, drink some coffee and sit out front with Juan while I get dinner ready." Juanita was excited to have a visitor and show off her new cabin. Little Juan and Hector were peeking around the corner of the door to see if it was ok to come out and see me. I pulled them both onto my lap and they started telling me all about their new home.

"Where's Tony?" I asked.

"He should be back sometime tomorrow. He was moving the cattle to new grass in the higher meadows. We need to save the lower grass for winter: Juan said. "I should have the roof on in a week or so and then I will start to cut some hay to feed this winter."

"All the supplies we got from the widow Smith have worked out well. We have only had to buy some small items from the store and Juanita is selling some pots she makes to cover most of the other supplies we need.

"Juanita," Ronnie asked, "tell me about the baskets and how you learned to make those pots."

"Well," she said, "when I was a little girl in California, our rancho had a river not too far from the house. The woman who looked after me during the day used to take me with her to get clay and reeds from the river bank.. I liked to watch the women make the baskets. We would sit on the back porch and they would weave them so I tried making them myself. The clay was worked until it had just the right feel, then one of the women would spin them on a kind of wheel. That was fun for a young girl. I learned over the years how to paint them and then place them in the oven to harden them."

"Juan made me an oven and a wheel so now I have fun making different designs. I found some clay by the stream on one of my walks. So most days I work the clay and make the pots to sell at Mr. Brown's store, then he pays me when he sells them. Mr. Brown told me that it is hard to keep any on his shelves.

Ronnie said to Juanita "You do great work." Then he turned to Juan and asked, "Juan, I need to ask you about something. How would you feel about me asking Tony to help take the horses back to Smith Creek Station?"

Juan replied "You take him. He is your age, he'll do a good job."

"Ok. In the morning we will go out and look over the horses. Do you think Tony's horse is up to the travel or do we need to get one of the mares for him to ride?"

Juan said, "No, he is fine with his horse. We just shoed him, he'll be fine."

Dinner was great. It was nice to just sit back and eat with friends. I told Juanita that I had met a young lady by the name of Abby. She works at Buckland Station on the Carson River and we have talked a bit. Her folks are both dead. They were killed on her trip out from back east. She is a strong girl like you.

"Can you believe it?" She drove the four horse team all the way from east of Salt Lake City to Buckland Station by herself. She was only 15 years old at the time. When I eat she comes in and sits with me and we talk. She even came out to the river and sat with me for a while before I came back here. Some time I will get her to tell me about her trip west. That had to be a hard trip on her being alone and all. It is still hard on me sometimes when I think back about Ma and Pa."

It was getting late so I said I was going out and sleep under the wagon and would see them in the morning. When I woke up the next day, I smelled bacon and coffee. It took a minute to remember I was at the ranch and Juanita must be cooking breakfast.

I could get used to this kind of life real fast. Walking down to the stream I washed off the sleep. Getting back up to the house Juanita said, "come eat - it's on the table." Steaming hot coffee and a plate of bacon, biscuits with honey, what could have been better to start the new day?

Juanita said "I asked Mr. Brown at the store to see if he could get some chickens so we could have eggs. He said he would if I sold him the extra eggs when we came to the store. He is supposed to have them when we go to the store next month. We will have a chicken coop ready by then."

After breakfast I looked around a mite to see how Juan had placed the house. I was surprised when I found a door leading out the back of the house. When I opened it I was looking into the dug-out. Juan said, "With the water seep coming into the dug-out we wanted to have a ready supply of water. Juanita placed a big clay pot to collect it.

Juanita said, "Now I never need to go to the stream."

Juan added, "If we get attacked we don't have to go out for water either." He was making a nice place to live for his family.

Tony rode in kicking up a little dust and was surprised to see me. I asked him how the grass was in the high meadows and could it carry the stock ok. Tony replied "It's real good. We will never even touch most of the grass with so few cows. They are getting fat."

I asked Tony, "how about you take a few days ride with me to deliver some horses?"

"Let's go – if it's alright with Juan," he said.

"So if you want to go, you need to get your kit ready for the trail. We will head back to Applegate's this afternoon to pick up the ten horses I just purchased."

I turned to Juan and said "let's get out and look over the horses around here." They were in a feeder canyon about a mile from the house. With the location of the ranch headquarters, we had four canyons we could hold the horses close in. We rode up and Diamond came to my call. You could see his muscles flexing under his coat. Man he looked great. After a little rubbing he went back to his job, watching his mares. I turned to Juan and said, "I think he likes his job, what do you think?." "Si, he is one proud horse!"

Tony was ready when we got back, with his saddle bags on and with the little kids on his horse. Tony was leading them around. I said good by to Juanita and the kids. Turning, we rode off down the canyon to pick up the ten horses from Sam.

I told Tony "I want to get a good part of the way back to Sam's place today so we would ride late. We need to pick the horses up and be on the way by noon." We made a cold camp, and were back up with first light. We came in to the Applegate's to find the horses with rope halters and tied together with lead ropes. They were ready to travel.

I traded saddles back to Buster and Lighting. Sam handed me the bill of sale for the ten horses and we headed down the trail. As we were turning, Sam called out his thanks for helping him out by buying the horses. With a wave of my arm we were making dust. We had three saddled horses and only two riders so we could trade off when needed. Dropping out of the hills we turned off southwest without going to Mr. Brown's Store.

Chapter 16 JON DUGAN'S RIDE INTO HELL

Victor Morales was the youngest son of Don Jose Morales, one of the largest land owners around Sacramento. His rancho was located fifty miles south and east of Sacramento. The land to the east had rolling hills and a large river cut across the ranch.

Victor had just found out that his older brother was in jail in Sacramento for shooting an unarmed man in a saloon. Victor had been to visit his brother in jail and talked to Sheriff Johnson about the case. Mr. Johnson had suggested that he go and talk to a lawyer in town who had just started his practice. Mr. Smith, the lawyer, told Victor that he would defend his brother but in the end his brother would hang. There were just too many people that had seen the shooting and the other man was unarmed.

Victor also talked to the lawyer about the stolen cattle and about the money the saloon owners Mr. Harding and Mr. Stanton cheated his brother out of during the last year. Victor set up another meeting with Mr. Smith the following week to look into the theft of the cattle and check brands on cattle on a ranch owned by Harding and Stanton.

Meanwhile, Jon Dugan had been pushing his horse hard for a few days. He had lost the posse that had been chasing him a few days back and was riding along, heading into Sacramento.

Looking ahead, he saw a man riding toward him heading south. This guy just rode right on by Jon on his big palomino stallion. The guy never even waved when Jon had said hi. Jon had heard the man call his horse Teddy as he clicked him up into a trot. This man was just not sociable, so Jon pulled his pistol and shot him right out of the saddle.

Jon said to himself. "Teddy, that is a good name for my new horse. That guy doesn't need him any more."

Jon went through the rider's pockets and found a letter from Juanita Lopez in Nevada addressed to Victor Rodrigo Morales, Stockton, California. Tossing it aside, he pulled out two hundred dollars in gold and put it in his own pocket. Jon then mounted the palomino and rode east toward Carson City.

Teddy was a prized stallion from the best breeding stock in California; he could cover some ground and was a real looker. Jon was wise to not leave any tracks that could be followed. After the shooting he backtracked for a few miles until he found a sand wash heading east toward the hills. Jon stopped long enough to brush out his tracks when entering the wash that would make it hard to follow him.

When heading east, Jon dropped out in front of a few hundred head of cattle being driven east. This herd would cover any trail he left.

Later that day when Jon stopped for some supplies at a trading post, a rancher asked if his horse was for sale. Jon told him "he had raised him from a colt and no thanks." Leaving the trading post he headed over the Sierras toward Carson City.

Just before dark Jon found a stream with some cover to make a camp for the night. Teddy needed some feed and rest. Jon had bought some oats for Teddy at the trading post earlier that day. Jon put Teddy on a picket within reach of good grass and water. He would be ready to make a hard ride in the morning. The two of them would need to spend another night in the mountains before reaching Carson City.

Late the second day he could see town. With some money in his pocket he decided to try his luck at a card table. Riding around behind the saloon, he tied Teddy to a hitch rail and headed in to get a drink and then he would play some cards.

Lady luck was not on his side. He had been losing almost every hand, then adding the five or six drinks he had downed, he was losing his money fast. After only two hours he was down to his gun belt and horse so he walked away broke.

Jon Dugan had just lost all of his traveling money to this slick gambler in Carson City. Jon had given some thought about pulling iron on him, but the gambler looked like he could shoot and shoot fast. Jon eased out the door of the saloon and waited just outside with his back to the wall. He waited for the gambler to walk out heading for dinner.

Jon had heard the gambler say he was about ready to go to dinner down the street, and he felt he would not need to wait long to get back his money and he hoped a lot extra.

He had his Navy Colt ready and cocked. When the gambler cleared the door, Jon pulled the trigger. He now had the money. Wrong! One of the local ranchers was stepping out right behind the gambler.

When the rancher heard the shot, he pulled his pistol and stepped out onto the porch. Jon turned, trying to face the new man, when the rancher lowered the gun, aiming it at him. Jon spun, turning to the left, just as the bullet whipped by his head into a wooden post holding up the roof. Jon snapped off a shot that hit the doorway as the rancher had ducked back inside just in time.

Jon ran around the corner to his palomino stallion and headed out of town. Now he had no money and had just killed a man. He felt the only chance he would have is to make a run to the east. Because the Indian war was going on, people would hesitate to follow him too far. East would be the best way to escape.

He either had to deal with the Indians or face a rope if he headed in any other direction. Having been chased before, he turned up the Carson River like he was going to California but after about three miles he went into the river to cover his tracks. After a mile or so he found a cut leading out of the river heading east. Then he kept in the soft sand as long as he could to help slow down anyone coming after him.

Jon was talking to himself and thinking how he could get any money in a hurry. He remembered hearing about a small trading post along the Carson River called Dayton Stage Stop that also served as the Pony Express station. He circled back behind a small mountain and re-crossed the river leading into Dayton.

He would be getting there late, and hoped no one would be around when he rode in, but the owner was walking out, ready to close when Jon rode in and said "Say mister, I need a few supplies. Can you help me out today?"

"Well, ok" he said, opening the door for him to enter. Jon walked in and the last thing the owner remembered was being hit on the head.

With some supplies and fifty dollars from the store owner's pocket, he was ready to head east again. As Jon started to walk out the door he noticed a new Henry rifle on the rack. He picked it up and also a couple hundred rounds of ammunition. Walking out to his horse, he pulled out the Spencer from his scabbard and shells from the saddle bags and replaced them on the rack inside the trading post. Jon thought "I wonder how he will like the trade and his sore head when he wakes up?"

He now had to make some time and get out of the area fast. His only problems could come at Fort Churchill and Buckland Station, but he felt no one could get there before he did. Jon rode all night to get past the last stop at the Carson River crossing. Once he got past there, no one would chase him in to the heart of the Pah Ute Indian war. Teddy was about worn out so he let him have a drink from the river and Jon filled his canteen. Coming out of the water, he headed down the Pony Express Trail. The mountains to the east were starting to show some light. Jon knew he had to get out of sight during the day.

A small draw opened up on his right side so he eased off the trail and down a sandy wash leading south, heading toward some low hills. He found a sheltered spot where he put his horse on a picket pin to graze.

The high bank offered a spot to take a nap in the shade. He didn't plan to get started east again until it was about dark. With some rest, and his horse fresh, he slipped along, going slow to keep his dust down. Even at night you could smell dust in the air. With a little moonlight he could tell there had been plenty of horse travel along the trail. Some looked like tracks from Indian ponies and some shod track that were probably Army horses from Fort Churchill.

After about six hours he was ready to find water for his horse so he started looking for one of the burned out Pony Express Stations. They all had some water. He felt that his luck had changed when he got the new Henry rifle. When he found the station empty he felt better about his choice of heading east to Salt Lake City.

Having found Hooten Wells clear and Sand Springs clear but just bad water, he moved on heading for Cold Springs. When he reached Cold Springs he still hadn't seen any Indians. What a run of luck he was having. Maybe he would just keep going on into Salt Lake and then see what he wanted to do.

Jon would pull out the new rifle and just look at it every so often. Robbing the Dayton Trading Post, getting the rifle and some cash had changed his luck, he had just known it as soon as he slid that rifle into his scabbard.

Getting away clean from the shooting at the saloon, getting a new rifle, and so far no problems with the Indians! He was also giving some thought about how lucky he had been to get this stallion from the man he had shot.

Jon felt that things were looking up for him. He was hoping to make big money with his next robbery. He just had to figure out who he would have to rob next. Jon was moving along real good and had cleared the last burned out Pony Express Station a few days ago, and Spring Creek Station was a day behind him now.

Jon knew he was clear of Indian trouble, and no posse would follow him. He had been riding slow, keeping an eye on his trail both in front and behind him. Looking ahead, he noticed some dust a few miles in front of him, coming his way. Jon eased Teddy off the trail behind some rocks and trees, and waited.

What luck! He had just about stopped at the little stream to camp tonight, but figured he would just make a few more miles before bedding down. He smiled "Oh my, look at this, two kids and thirteen horses. I have just had my luck get even better. I should be able to sell those horses for a lot of money in Salt Lake City. It was only a few days ride from here." Then he got a look at Lighting and Buster. Damn, all those horses were better than most he had seen in years. This would be a good payday.

He let the boys move along down the trail. When he felt that they had made about a mile he slipped out onto the trail, followed slowly, staying well back so not to be seen. Dark was coming fast and he could see they had stopped at the little stream. It was more of a seep than a stream.

Earlier he had watered Teddy there at the stream. He had seen a small trail leading back into the rocks and he was pretty sure that's where the two kids would camp tonight.

With his many years of sneaking around in the woods, he was sure he could slip up on them without them ever knowing. Jon waited about three hours until all was quiet. The only noises coming from the campsite were the horses cropping grass and a stomp of a hoof now and then.

*

Tony and I had made good time heading back to Smith Creek with the string of horses. He had five horses and I had six on the lead ropes. My plan was to send Tony home with some pocket money for his help on the trail. The first day we made good time even with the extra horses. We only stopped one time by a small stream to let the horses have a drink. With the sun going down I told Tony there was a good spot with some grass and a little water just up the trail about a mile.

I got the horses on grass and with water close. They would do just fine. I had Tony get the fire started and get some food ready. I wanted to take a look at our back trail. You never knew if you had picked up a problem.

Thirteen horses and only two men might make someone think they needed the horses and make a try for them. I had had a feeling late in the day that we are being dogged by someone. Just as the light was fading I got a look at a rider topping a small ridge and coming on slow. We had just been there an hour ago.

After watching the trail, Ronnie went back to camp. He told Tony that they may have some company after a few hours. "I spotted a rider moving up behind us. This may not be any problem, but we are not going to be caught flat footed either."

Ronnie asked Tony to build up the fire, then they placed both of their bedrolls beside the fire in plain view. "Now let's lay our two Sharps rifles down beside each of the bedrolls to make it look like we are asleep." said Ronnie.

Tony took a spot back from the fire in the trees to the left to wait. He had the two Navy Colt Pistols and he could shoot pretty good. During the trip I had him shoot my .44's a time or two for practice. I moved to the other side and out of Tony's line of fire so I could have a clear shot if need be.

Then we waited to see if trouble came our way. Anyone who was honest would call out to identify himself when he got close to the fire. If he did that it would be ok. But if he had other ideas, he was going to have a problem. In fact he would have two problems. I had Tony work at loading and shooting from horseback during this trip. Having this skill could save his life sometime. I felt sure he would shoot if needed and hit what he was shooting at.

As usual, I had gone out to watch the back trail just before sunset. I found the path that would lead from the trail coming in from the east. This path led right to the campsite. If a body had a mind to sneak up on us, this would be the way he would come in.

*

Jon was feeling good now. He couldn't see anyone sitting by the fire so they must have been tired and gone to bed early, he thought. Jon was coming in slow and quiet, just a little more. "Yeah" he said to himself. "Look at them damn kids, are just sleeping by the fire with no idea anyone is around."

Working another few feet, he thought he had a good shot at the two boys sleeping. Just let me help them into a long sleep, he smiled. This is going to be easy. He lifted his brand new rifle to his shoulder and took aim.

Jon Dugan pulled the trigger and levered a second shell into the chamber and fired the second round into the boys' beds. This was just too easy he said to himself.

Then he heard the sound coming from his right. He levered the action as he started to turn, too late. That's when he felt the bullet hit him just under the right shirt pocket and two more enter his back on the left side. "Damn them kids. Damn my luck anyway!"

When the shooting was over and the smoke cleared, I picked up a new log and put it on the fire so we could see a little better. Tony sat down on a log and looked up at me saying "he was going to kill us for the horses."

"Well it sure looked that way to me," I said. "I don't think he will try that again. What do you think?"

I asked Tony to go through his pockets and see if he had anything to tell us who he was. I eased back down the path the killer had come into camp on and picked up his horse. When bringing him back to camp I got a better look and could tell he was a fine looking animal. Pulling the saddle off, I could tell it was Spanish style, with some silver trim.

I told Tony that this drifter must have stolen the horse and outfit. "This horse is way out of that guy's class. Look, Tony, we will finish going through his stuff in the morning when we have better light. Let's get some sleep now."

Tony asked me. "How did you know he was up to no good?"

"Well, when I saw him coming along slow and it being a little late to make camp, it just didn't look good. I didn't know but I was not going to take a chance either. Pa told me so many times to keep track of your back trail. If we had just rolled up into our bedrolls we would be dead now."

"When you are taking a trip like this it pays to watch both ways, take your time along the trail so you don't ride into a problem you are not ready for." We pulled him back into the brush a bit, and then both moved our bedrolls back into the trees away from the fire. When I pulled the blanket over me I found a bullet hole with my finger. Thinking a bit on that, I pulled the blanket up and went to sleep. We slept a little later than usual and the sun was already up when I woke up.

After pulling on my boots I went over to the fire and added some small twigs to get it going. Coffee was boiling when Tony rolled out and came to the fire for a cup of coffee. After we ate I knew we had to go through this guy's stuff. In the left front pocket we found fifty dollars, but no way to identify him. After checking his saddle bags we went over to take a look at his horse.

"Tony, it looks like you have just got yourself a real nice stud. Is this trip working out for you ok so far? You now can start your own herd of horses." Ronnie continued "By the looks of this stuff he must have robbed someone. Man, look at your new horse and custom saddle. I wonder if we will ever find out anything about this man."

I told Tony to keep the fifty dollars and all of his equipment along with the Henry rifle. "It's a good one. It's like new and, in fact, it could not be over a few months old. What are we going to do with this guy?" The best we could do was move him to a dirt bank and push some over him. We didn't have a shovel so we put a few rocks on top to keep the animals out.

Getting out some of the food Juanita sent, we ate a bite, saddled up and got on our way, hopeful of no problems today.

We still had a two day ride to the Smith Creek Station, but we made it in without any more problems. We came in to the station at a hard trot with all of the horses trailing behind. I rode into the corral and started to turn them loose. "Say, Tony, fork up some hay and let's give them some grain if you can find any, will you? Tony, do you want to stay over or get headed back home?"

"I guess I will head home now if it's ok. I want to show Juan and Juanita this new horse, saddle and new Henry rifle." said Tony.

Ronnie reached into his pocket and pulled out some money to pay him for his work. Tony tried to not take the money but in the end he put it in his pocket. "Ronnie, do I really get this horse and gun as you said?"

"They are yours, and thanks for the help."

Tony turned and cantered back down the trail toward home, leading his old horse and sitting proud on his new golden stallion. He also knew a little more about life on the trail and he would also be watching his back trail during his ride home.

Mochila waiting for a ride. Picture by either Richard Massey, Sarah Morey, or Nick McCabe. Setting along the Carson River by Fort Churchill State Park.

Chapter 17 MEETING PONY BOB

When Ronnie walked into the station he met the crew that had been rebuilding the relay stations starting at Hooten Wells. "Well boys, are we getting ready to ride with some mail or we still on hold?" Andy Sams said. "Nah, Bolivar said for you to start dropping two horses at the small relay stations and three at the larger ones on your way back to Carson City." ,"Well" I said, "I will get some sleep and be off in the morning, heading west." Andy also told Ronnie that Bolivar is dropping some mounts he found, starting at Hooten Wells Station heading east. You should meet the other rider in a day or so and then you are both to head back to Carson together. "Andy, do you know who is coming this way?"

"No, we never talked about that. But he told me to not have you drop off Lighting or Buster. He wants them in Carson City."

The next morning, with the smell of bacon and hot coffee, Ronnie climbed down from the hay loft. He saddled Lighting and Buster and then lead them to the hitching rail. Ronnie would go back and pick up the other horses after he had a bite to eat. The food was good and when he finished eating and walked out on the porch he found all of the horses were ready to go. The young horse handler, Tim, said. "This is my job! I got them ready so you can get off any time you are ready."

Ronnie stepped up and turned west, leading off with the horses at a trot, making dust, heading for the next relay station and loving every minute of it.

What could be better than riding fast horses and getting paid to do it? He would need to ask Mr. Bolivar when he would get paid and did he get any extra for making the ride to pick up the horses at Sam's ranch.

Ronnie met the other guy who had been dropping horses heading east at Cold Springs Station a few days later. Ronnie had dropped his last two horses and the two riders, turned, and headed back to Carson City.

When they started cantering down the trail Ronnie said, "what is your name?"

He told Ronnie is name was Pony Bob. Ronnie told him, "I just missed you a few weeks ago at Spring Creek Station. You had just headed back a few hours before I came in with the other horses."

Bob said, "I should have waited. I could have had some fresh horses for my return trip."

Bob asked Ronnie why he was bringing two horses back to Carson City. He was riding Lighting right then so he told Bob to jump over onto Buster and give him a try. Bob handed him the reins to his horse and Buster was about four lengths ahead in about three jumps.

Ronnie had no chance to keep up because he had Bob's horse in tow. In a few minutes Bob pulled back and waited for Ronnie to catch up to him. When he rode up alongside Bob, he saw the big smile on his face. "Damn this horse is fast! I don't think I have ever ridden any horse as fast as this one."

Ronnie turned and told him that Lighting was only a nose slower and he could try him later.

They got talking about fast horses and that is when Ronnie told him he had ridden a stud that would outrun either of them, but it would still be a race. Bob asked, "where can I get a leg over that horse?"

Ronnie said "I was working on a ranch when I rode him and I don't think he is around any longer."

When we got close to Buckland and Fort Churchill I told Pony Bob I was going to stay at Buckland overnight and would come on in to Carson City in a day or so.

Bob said, "I will wait over at Fort Churchill for ya, I need to talk to the Station Manager anyway, so when you are ready, just ride on over and we can head out from there. I may have some fun waiting for you when you get there."

Chapter 18 RONNIE'S FIRST KISS

Ronnie turned onto Buckland and with a wave, Bob headed on down the trail to Fort Churchill to set up a little horse race. Bob knew that one of the officers, a Major, had a horse that had beat every horse in the area. He thought to himself that is going to change soon, and some money was going to also change hands.

Abby had seen Ronnie coming in and was waiting at the corral gate when he finished stripping the gear off the horses. Turning, he was greeted by a big smile and a wave. He walked over and opened the gate and Abby just stepped up and planted a little kiss right on his lips.

Ronnie asked if we could that again? Abby said, "I think we may do this more each time we see each other."

"I may just need to stop by each day! That was great."

Abby said, "just shut up and kiss me real good, and do your best this time." He was new at this, but was learning fast.

This was bringing up some new feelings in him, and he was getting hard as a rock. He was starting to push into Abby's belly. She could feel him through her dress and decided this was getting a little too warm for her. Abby said, "lets go and get you some food and we will take it out to the bank of the river. We can talk, eat, and kiss some. What do you think?"

"I am up to that and I do mean up."

"Abby, why don't you go get our food, I will grab my blanket and go out by the river and wait for you." On the way to the river, Ronnie was telling himself I think she likes me, well damn, I know she likes me.

In a bit Abby was back with the food and she did it again. She just walked in and started kissing him. He was doing his best to keep up with her but was feeling himself getting hard again.

Abby said, "you don't need to be shy. I know a little about your problem, and it's ok. Let's sit down so we can eat, its been a long day and you have had a hard ride."

Abby said, "look Ronnie, I like you and I think you like me. We are going to be doing a lot of kissing, but I am not ready to go much further until we know each other better. I knew if I waited on you we would be holding hands for a year.

"Ok let's talk some" Ronnie said. "When do you want to tell me all about your trip west and ending up at Buckland Station? I know you have had a hard time and I really do like you too and I want to know all about you and where you came from."

Abby said, I think I'm ready now and this will take some time. Do you know that I lived in Pennsylvania in the small town of Wellsboro? It is in the northern part of the state.

My full name is Abigail Combs. My mom was Wilda Combs and dad was Lee Combs. They had the general store in Wellsboro for many years.

Dad met a man, Chet Roe, who had traveled to California by wagon train many years before. After hearing about the open country, Dad and Mom both decided to go west to St Louis and connect with a wagon train heading to California.

Dad just hated it when the civil war started and he wanted to get out of Pennsylvania to a fresh new land. Dad and Mom talked to Chet for many days about all of what we would need to make the trip.

Chet and Dad made a list of equipment we would need to work a ranch. Most of the supplies we would need we already had in the store. Dad and Chet made a box the size of a wagon to see just how big of a wagon we would need. They stacked the heavy equipment on the bottom and when this was done then packed things we would need to build the house and barn. The last thing they worked on was a place for them to sleep and in the front a bed for me.

Dad went to the wagon maker in town to have him make him a custom wagon just like the big box they had used. Chet had told Dad to have this wagon built with wider wheels so it would pull better in soft sand.

Dad then went out to find the four horses we would need to pull our new wagon. Dad knew a horse trader named Dill Goodwin. He was supposed to know every horse in four counties.

After a couple of weeks Dill rode over and told Dad to mount up and come take a look at some horses. When Dad came back he had five great big draft horses. Dad had purchased four mares and a stallion. Dad had a way with horses and this big stallion was real gentle, even I could handle him.

Dill told Dad that the stallion was always hitched in the lead on the right front side of the team. He would not work any other place. Dad and Dill worked the team for a couple of day just to make sure they would work well together. Dad used a friend's wagon and loaded it with rocks to see what his new team could pull.

We had a long hill just outside of town and Dad and Dill took the load of rocks up to the top without any problems. They also decided that a better test would be to see if the team would hold the load coming back down. That is a true test, when they started back down all four horses just about sat down holding the load. We now knew we had a team that could make the long trip to California.

Mom and Dad sold the store to a new man in town at a good price. Dad sold our house to a widow lady for a rooming house. We were now ready to go anytime the wagon was finished.

Our new wagon arrived in a couple of weeks and with all of the equipment loaded we said our goodbyes and left town heading west with three horses on lead ropes; the extra draft horse and two saddle horses.

Dad had all of the heavy equipment loaded on the bed of the wagon and the next layer had some of the things Mom felt we could not do without. Most of these were special household items. They were stacked up to the top of the tarp that covered the bed of the wagon.

In the front and back Dad made two beds with household things in between their bed and mine. I had a small place to sleep just behind the wagon seat.

Abby turned to Ronnie and said. "That's how I knew about your problem because of sleeping that close to Mom and Dad. I kind of learned some things about what married folks do. Are you doing better now?"

"Yes" he said. "Tell me some more about your trip."

"Well, ok,. the two saddle horses we were leading behind the wagon were both Saddle Bred geldings. You may have seen them in the corral behind the station. I take them out for a ride sometimes."

"Mr. Buckland is using my draft horses until I need them. He would like to buy them from me but I don't want to sell them until I know what I am going to do. I've got to tell you Ronnie, I loved the trip to St. Louis. It was just great. We had a lot of snow and bad weather but the team just moved right along. We traveled over the winter so we could be in St Louis ready to travel west with the first wagon train in early spring."

"We arrived with just enough time to stock up with supplies for the trip west. The wagon master, Bob Stanton, took dad's money and checked out our wagon. He told Dad it was a good wagon and built to last and he liked the wider wheels. The next day we started west with about fifteen other wagons of all shapes and sizes. Only two were larger than ours."

"I remember Dad saying we would have a problem with the two larger wagons because they only had two draft horses pulling them. The teams would have a tough time pulling those big wagons in the soft sand country. Most of the wagons were pulled by oxen. Oxen were slow, but after watching them during the trip, I saw they never quit just plodding along day after day.

Mom and I walked much of the way to help save the horses. Dad let me ride the geldings sometimes. I got to know Bob Stanton, the wagon master, quite well when riding during the first few weeks. He would drop back and talk to us about the trip ahead.

After Mr. Stanton watched me ride for a few days, I asked him if he would let me ride with the scout, Joe Harding. Bob said ok. That was great fun. We would swing wide and range way out in front of the wagon train to check for places with water and good grass to stop at night. Joe Harding told me if we had any problems with Indians, I was to turn and run flat out back to the wagon train and don't look back.

We were having a great trip and making good time until we got to Indian country. We had to be a little more cautious and started to set out guards each night. We all had to stay close to the wagons and have our rifles ready at all times.

The morning of the attack I woke up early hearing Mom and Dad making some noise and talking low. I knew they were making love. I just laid there being quiet and thinking. After they finished Dad got up and heated some water then handed Mom the bucket with warm water for her to wash up with.

Then Mom asked if I was awake and wanted to wash up a bit. I got up and joined her. Then we all started getting ready to move out. I had just climbed back in the wagon and was rolling up my bed when the Indians attacked. I was behind the wagon seat when they came at us yelling and shooting at the wagons.

I pulled out Dad's rifle from beside the wagon seat and started shooting. I know the first shot killed one and I think I hit two more. Soon everybody was shooting. We killed about ten or so, then they turned and rode away. I climbed down off the wagon and Mom was dead, laying beside one of the horses.

Dad had an arrow in his shoulder. The scout came over to help Dad back inside of the wagon circle. He then took a look at the arrow. The arrow head had not gone all the way out his back, so Mr. Harding broke off the arrow leaving about two inches sticking out the front. Then he told me to get a stick for Dad to bite down on.

He told Dad to look at me. When he did, Mr. Stanton hit the end of the arrow with his rifle butt and pushed it the rest of the way through so he could pull the shaft out. He said to get some medicine and bandage up the wound, we needed to get on the road soon.

I had been lucky being in the wagon with the seat for protection. Dad and Mom had been working on the outside two horses hooking up the tugs to the double tree when the Indians attacked.

They didn't have a chance to get away. I don't think I would have ever made it through the day without Mr. Stanton's and Mr. Harding's help. They took over for me and dug the grave and had Mom wrapped in a blanket in no time.

I was just able to stand when they read over Mom from the Bible. Dad was hardly able to sit in a chair at that time, he was hurt so bad. I do hope to see Mr. Harding & Mr. Stanton again some time so I can tell them just how much help they were to me in my time of need.

I doctored Dad for the next two weeks but it was no good. He died just outside Salt Lake City. Mr. Stanton and Mr. Harding stepped in again to get Dad buried. I felt bad that Mom was buried a long way from Dad but there was little I can do about it. I had been lucky that Dad had let me drive the team some of the trip before he was killed.

I have got to say my hands were about ready to bleed. Dad's gloves were too big, but I made do, but everything was sure sore the first days. By the time we got into Salt Lake City my hands were better, and I was handling the wagon just fine. I did have some help from a couple of the boys who were on the wagon train with us. They kind of quit though after I would'nt do any sparking with them. They sure wanted me to let them kiss me.

"You let me kiss you and you kiss me back." I said.

Abby said: "Yeah, but I like you." When the wagon train pulled into Buckland Station I just felt that I was in a place I needed to be. So I made a deal with Mr. Buckland to stay on and work for room and board. That is how I got to Buckland Station. "Now will you kiss me or do I have to do all the work? Although, if this is work, let me be overworked."

It was getting dark when they walked back to the station. Abby said, "let's stop at the corrals and look over my horses." When Abby walked up to the corral the big stallion walked over for his rub. "Look at the two big Standard Bred geldings and tell me what you think."

"They look like they can run," Ronnie said. "When you get a chance let's take them out and just see how fast they are." Then he continued, "look, you know I need to get on to Carson City in the morning don't you?"

"Yeah, but you will be back to see me soon, right?"

"Yes, I will need some more work on this kissing stuff." Ronnie smiled.

Abby went back to her room and Ronnie climbed the ladder to the hay loft, laying awake for thinking about how Abby would fit in with his ranch plans. He was also thinking she would fit just fine in other places. He was still thinking about her when he drifted of to sleep.

Chapter 19 BUSTER GETS A RACE

Ronnie could smell the bacon cooking and he was ready to eat a big breakfast. He also wanted to talk to Abby before he had to ride over to Fort Churchill and meet Pony Bob for the ride on in to Carson City. After breakfast Abby went to the corral when Ronnie got saddled and she gave him a going away kiss that he felt all the way to Fort Churchill.

Ronnie came into the fort at a stiff trot, leading Buster. Bob was waiting on the porch of the settlement store with his feet resting on the top railing. Pony Bob looked like he was not in any hurry to get started so Ronnie stepped down and walked up to the porch and took a seat beside him.

"Well Bob, are we going or what?"

Bob said, "we have a small job to do first, and then we will head to Carson with some of the Army's money in our pockets.

Bob said "I just was talking about how fast Buster was, and damn if one of the officers didn't walk up and he tell me that no horse could beat his in a race. Well, you kind of get the drift. I think we should just take a little time to relieve the men in blue from their money. In fact they are getting their pot together now. How much do you have on you? You could say I'm a little light, I only have a dollar on me right now. Can you cover a little bet with what you have on you?"

"So let me get this right, you set this race up, then you want to use my money to cover the bet and then you want me to split the winnings."

Bob said, "that is about it. Let's walk over to take a look at the horse you are going to beat."

We headed over to the stable to take a look-see. By the time we got there everyone who could walk was standing around this big blood bay. He must have stood well over sixteen hands.

Bob said, "Well boys, what is this little race going to cost us to cover your bet, we have a hundred dollars.

The major said "You will need to match that if you want to run your horse."

Old Bob just looked at me with eyes saying get our money out and cover the bet or let's ride. This bet was going to be a minor problem. He knew I had fifty dollars left from the cattle sale and a couple nuggets in my pocket.

Ronnie thought: Now, how do I deal with the gold nuggets without being asked a lot of questions? Then he said, "Look, lets do this, I have some money but not enough to cover the bet, but also I have a couple of gold nuggets my dad left me when he died. I will take them into the settlers store and see what they will give me for the two nuggets. I will be back in a bit."

On the way to the store he pulled out two from his bag and pocketed them. When he got to the counter he asked the owner to weigh the two nuggets to see how much they were worth.

"Look son, they come to twenty five each."

Ronnie said, "ok, give me fifty now and if I win the race I will come back and pick up the nuggets, that is all I own in the world."

"All right son, I will hold them till after the race."

Ronnie took the fifty dollars and walked back to the stable to cover the bet.

Bob was smart, he knew if the race was too long that big Thoroughbred would win. Bob had one of the other Pony Express riders, a guy named Larry McPherson, set up the race course,

Bob had him move a wagon down the road just about a quarter mile for the turn around point, so the riders would go down and turn around the wagon and head for home. They all wanted the finish line right here in front of the main gate, so everyone could see the finish of the race. That gave Ronnie the edge: He knew Buster could turn faster than the big bay. By the time Ronnie got back to the store Bob had the saddle bags off and about everything else he could take off and still call it a saddle.

Bob was a good bit of a trickster. He also talked them into a standing start. I was beginning to think Bob may just earn his part of the pot if Buster could only do his job now.

We got lined up and both of us were ready. Bob raised his pistol and pulled the trigger. Both horses were off. I got the jump and was moving ahead but I could hear that big bay coming on fast, so I let Buster have his head. To my surprise he was holding the bay off. When we got to the wagon for the turn, I came to a sliding stop making the turn for home. That big bay took a few more strides to make it around the turn and I had him by about four lengths. Now would be the test.

I did not need to tell Buster he had a race on his hands. That bay edged up and his nose was even with my knee now and we still had a long way to go. I think Buster got a look at that bay and it wasn't to his liking. He just stretched out and moved away. When we got to the finish line we had a good two lengths lead.

When I got back to the store, Bob had given the store owner the money back for my nuggets and had all of the cash. He then started counting out the money, looking up and said, "one for me and one for you how about that."

We now have some spending money, or I should say Bob now had some spending money, I had some already.

While Bob was putting back all the stuff he had taken off Buster's saddle, I talked to Major Smith, the owner of the big bay. I told him about getting the horses past the Indians. He asked me about the water I had found during my rides across. He said it was good to know because he may need it some time when out on patrol.

He told me this was the only time his horse had lost a race in his life.

I told him about having to outrun the Indians on my trip east. Major Smith thought that by changing out between the two horses it had made the difference and allowed me to get away. I said Lighting and Buster were the difference. Then I told him that Lighting was only a nose slower than Buster.

The major said, "You tell Bolivar Roberts if he ever wants to sell those two horses I will buy them just for myself to ride."

Ronnie suggested "When you get the Indians under control, why don't you see if you can recover some of the grays that Bolivar Roberts purchased for the Pony Express last year and return them."

He said, "If we find any we will do just that."

Walking away, I turned and said thanks for the money. Pony Bob had everything ready so we just stepped up and turned toward Carson City. After a ways Bob turned and said, "I think Buster can beat that bay in a fair race what do you think?

"Yes I do think so too, he is one fast horse."

Chapter 20 MEETING WHITE BIRD

Juan was working in the high country checking on the stock when he came upon a dead Indian pony. The pony had a broken front leg and its throat had been cut.

Looking a little closer he could see drag marks leading into some timber and rocks. Pulling out his Henry he eased up to the rocks looking around to see if the rider had just been hurt or killed. Behind a big bolder he found the Indian. He looked about as bad as his horse did. Juan could tell he was hurt bad. He could see a broken leg and forearm on the same side. There was no way to tell how long he had been laying there. Juan went back to his horse to get his canteen. Checking the Indian for weapons, Juan removed his knife. Then he washed the Indian's face and got a little water down him. Juan knew the Indian would die if he didn't stay there for a couple of days. He figured that when the horse went down it rolled over him, breaking his leg and arm. If he was hurt badly inside he would die soon.

After a bit he got some more water down him. If he was going to live he would need plenty of water and some meat. Juan gathered some wood and built a fire and put a blanket over the Indian to keep him warm.

Now he had to set the leg and arm. A small stream was close so he cut some willow sticks, then pulled the leg back in place the best he could. After the leg looked straight, he placed the sticks around the leg and bound it with leather strips he had in his saddle bags. Then Juan went to work on the Indian's arm. Juan was glad the Indian had passed out from the pain, so he worked fast to finish the job while he was still out cold.

Juan was not partial to horse meat but it was close and he was hungry. Cutting off some meat, he put it on a stick to cook over the fire

Then he went out and filled his frying pan with some water and added some of the meat he had cooked to make broth to feed his new friend. Now the 'friend' part he would need to wait and see how that worked out.

I wonder who he is? I know he is a Pah Ute by the bead work on his buckskin shirt. Looking at his shirt, Juan could see a picture of a bird outlined in white beads. "I will call him White Bird!"

When the Indian came around, the looks Juan got were not all that friendly. Juan wished Tony was back from his trip but he knew it would be a few days yet even if he had come straight back without stopping any place to spend some of his money he earned.

Juanita would be having a fit by now, it was getting dark and he would not be going home tonight. Women just seem to get worked up when they don't know what is going on, he thought.

If this Indian lived till morning he would give him some meat and water, then head back to the ranch to pick up another horse for the Indian. Juan figured he would sleep back away from the fire a ways, so not to give the Indian any ideas of trying to kill him.

Juan was lying back, leaning on his saddle, thinking this high country is so filled with stars. The moon was full tonight and it looked like you could see forever in the dim light. Being over ten thousand feet up it seemed that you are lying under a blanket of stars. You could almost reach out and touch them. I wonder if the Indian liked to look at the night sky. Juan was thinking about that when he went to sleep.

The sun was coming up as Juan walked back to the fire and put some wood chips on the coals to get the fire going again. The Indian looked kind of mean still. Walking up to him, Juan squatted down in front of the fire and pointed to the Indian saying "White Bird" Then pointing to himself, he said "Juan."

With the fire going, he put some more of the horse meat on to cook and gave the Indian some water, he looked like he would live. Just before he left for the ranch he pulled in some wood so White Bird could just push it into the fire with his good arm to keep warm.

Juan felt it would be a good idea if he kind of kept at a distance until they got to know each other a little better. He didn't think the Indian spoke any English, so he took a stick and made a little picture on the ground showing him going and coming back with a horse. Leaving some cooked meat and water, Juan headed home to pick up a horse.

When he rode into the yard Juanita came running out of the house with the kids right behind her. "I was so scared" she said, "I thought you were hurt. When will Tony be back?" she asked?

After she calmed down, Juan told her about the Indian friend and his dead horse, then about setting his broken arm and leg.

Juanita said with her eyes wide, "You don't go back by yourself. When Tony gets back, then you go."

Juan went out and put up his horse and fed the other stock. Juanita had said that dinner would be ready in a little while if he promised to stay close to the house until Tony returned.

When he finished, the sun was down and he headed back to the house to eat. Little Juan and Hector were all over his lap making it hard to eat. Life was good. Juanita came to bed ready for things other than sleep saying we needed to work on getting a little girl. That's why you need to wait until Tony gets back.

The sun was about up when Juanita rolled over placing her hand on him and asked if they could finish what they started last night.

"I think you can tell I am up to it, breakfast can wait." Juan said.

After breakfast he was getting ready to finish feeding the stock. when he heard hoof beats. Who could be coming to the ranch this early in the morning? Big as life, Tony came riding in on the best looking palomino Juan had ever seen. He called Juanita to get out here. Tony was back! She came out onto the porch and just fainted dead away.

We got her back into the house and started washing her face, she started to cry and was saying my "My brother, my brother."

"Juanita, calm down what is wrong? Tell us."

"That is my brother Victor's horse Teddy. He raised him on the rancho in California up by Sacramento. How did you get him?"

Tony sat down and told of the man trying to kill Ronnie and him on the way to deliver the horses. "This man shot into our blankets trying to kill us, we shot and killed him. Ronnie gave me the horse and his Henry rifle, that is all I know."

Juanita said, "Juan, I need to send a letter to the rancho telling of the horse. I feel my younger brother was killed by that man you killed. Go and look under the saddle, you will find my brother's letters VM burned into the saddle skirt. I know that horse and saddle. It's my brother's, Victor Morales. Stripping off the saddle, on the skirt were the initials VM.

"Juanita, are you going to be all right? We need to go and get a horse up to that Indian in the mountains, Tony can come and help me. We will be back in a day or two."

Juanita said "I will be ok, maybe it will be better if I am alone for a day or two anyway." "Go. I can't just let him lay there and die, so yes I am ok."

Tony told Juan if you are going to give the Indian a horse, you know you will never get it back. Tony said, "let's give him my other horse. He is not the best, and we have better horses, what you say.?"

"Ok, pull off your saddle and we will do that. The Indian's horse only had a bridle and no saddle, so that idea will work just fine.

They headed back to the high country to get the Indian on a horse and let him go home if he could. They told each other "We will have done all we could for him."

Later that day, they got back to the Indian and he was still looking bad, but was sitting up. They got some wood and cooked some dinner and they all ate. The Indian didn't look so mean this time. Tony and Juan would wait out the night and get him on the horse in the morning and see if he could ride without help.

With the sun coming up they fixed a bit to eat and helped the Indian onto the horse. Juan gave him back his knife and tied a sack of jerky to the horse's mane. Juan then gave him a canteen with fresh water. Tony traded out the bridle and they sent him on his way. Whether he would make it back they would never know.

Tony said, "Let's head home. I think Juanita wants to go to Mr. Brown's store to mail that letter to her family in California.

Chapter 21 WHITE BIRD'S RIDE TO HIS VILLAGE

White Bird rode off slowly with his broken leg and arm. He was in a lot of pain as he rode north, leaving the two men who had saved his life behind. They watched as he topped the rise going out of sight. White Bird wondered why did they help me? Why did they let me go? Maybe they will follow me hoping I will lead them to the village. Do they know that I was one of the war party that attacked the man by the cabin?

What a battle. We lost five braves before killing the white man. He fought well and his rifle could shoot many times. My wife's brother, Big Soldier, had the honor of making the shot that killed him and then he took the rifle.

White Bird rode toward his village, taking it slowly so not to fall off his horse. Each step made his leg hurt. After a while he turned into the trees running along the base of the mountain. He worked his way along, riding on the pine needles to lose his tracks. He doubled back and made a false trail leading out into the valley again. Then he rode into the stream bed to cover his tracks.

Riding in the stream bed for about a mile, he found a rock outcropping leading back to the timber. He used the rocks to cover his tracks leading out of the stream. The only way anyone could see that he left the stream were some water drops on the rocks. This rock outcropping led him back into the trees and onto the pine needles again and onto the old trail leading up and over the mountain.

Using his good hand, he held onto the horse's mane to keep from sliding off. The climb was steep, so every time he found a level spot he would let the horse blow and catch his breath. White Bird was glad to have a rest also.

Reaching the pass leading over the mountain took most of the day. White Bird would need to find a spot to spend the night soon. As the light was starting to fade, he made it to a little spring that had some grass and trees for cover to crawl under to spend the night.

Riding under a tree, he was able to grab on with his good arm so he could lift his good leg over the horse's back, then slide down the horse's side to get his weight on the good foot. Untying the jerky from the mane, he worked himself over to the pool of water.

He let his horse drink, then he worked back under the trees to sleep. Later he woke up and ate some of the jerky and drank from the canteen the two men had given to him.

He wondered again why the white men had not killed him. First light found him cold but alive. Now he had to find a way to get back onto the horse. He found a rock with a tree growing along side of it. Crawling over to the rock and getting hold of tree branch, he got himself standing. White Bird now needed to get up onto the rock. Holding onto a limb with his good arm, he was able to pull up. Working his horse over beside the rock, he now was able to get his broken leg over the horse's back. With a lot of pain he was able to slide in place.

Sweat was running when he finished getting aboard. Pulling himself in place by using his horse's mane, he was finally ready to go. Turning back onto the trail, he headed north again following the dim trail leading along the face of the mountain.

This trail has been used by his tribe for as long as anyone could remember. It was a war trail used when they went raiding to the south. White Bird remembered Big Soldier had been missing for a long time now. His horse had come back to the village without his rider. Everyone thought that Big Soldier must have been killed."

White Bird now worked his way down out of the mountains. The riding was easier now with less climbing. His arm hurt, and his leg was making it hard to stay on the horse. Having no choice other than to stay on and ride or die, he kept his horse moving. Stopping after a while, he got out another piece of the jerky and tried to take his mind off of his broken leg. He would be able to make it to his village by the time the sun went behind the mountain today.

As the sun started to set, White Bird rode by a small river as it wound around the valley floor heading to his village. The sun dropped over the hills just as White Bird rode into his summer home. His brother Tee came out to help him down from the horse. His wife ran in and made a soft bed of firs to lie on. They had started to think he was lost like Big Soldier. White Bird told his brother he would have to start hunting for two families for a while now, for Big Soldier's family and our own.

As his leg started to heal Tee and White Bird sat by the fire talking about the white men who gave him the horse and why did they not kill him. Are they weak and afraid? The one said his name was Juan and didn't seem afraid. He took my knife but gave it back. They gave me a horse so I could ride back here to the village.

"They fixed my leg and arm, gave me food to eat on my way home. I don't understand them. We made a war raid and killed the man at the cabin, but they still saved my life." White Bird said.

When my leg gets better we will ride back to the mountain with the yellow rock and watch to see what they do. Two moons later White Bird and Tee set off to ride back down the war trail to the place with the yellow rock to watch the men.

After riding around the mountains, they found a big stallion with about twenty mares in a back canyon. They watched this stallion and the man who watched the cows for days. White Bird told Tee he was going to bring some of their mares to breed with this stallion.

They watched the man move the cows from one little valley to another. This man would watch the cows until they started to eat and go to water. Then he would go to another valley and do the same. One time they had ridden out of a stream bed and crossed to the next hill before the man came with the cows. The man watching the cows saw the tracks and pulled his rifle and sat watching. After the cows got settled he put the rifle back and rode off down the canyon.

After a few moons, White Bird and Tee had seen enough and started home. They needed to have some time to think and plan what they wanted to do next. Many of their tribe had been killed by the soldiers from the fort by the river. "To fight them is not good, we are too few."

During the ride back to their camp the two brothers talked about what they had seen. They talked about trying to see if they could change how they lived to protect their families. Many of the other braves still wanted to kill the white men. Each council was held by the elders. The two brothers sat quietly and listened to the others speak.

Big Soldier never came home but his horse had and many moons had passed, so he must be dead. He had been the leader of this band, now they would need to pick another to take his place. White Bird and Tee had moved Big Soldier's wife, Moon Glow, into there lodge for her protection and to provide food for her and her two young children. Tee and White Bird talked about Tee taking her for his wife but was not sure yet what to do. Moon Glow would not take another man for another two moons, but she was looking at Tee all the time.

The two Indians were hunting all of the time to build up supplies of meat. Their plan was starting to come together. White Bird and Tee decided to go back to the mountain of gold and see if they could help the man with the cows. They would try to change the way they lived just to see if an Indian could live without raiding and killing. To do this they would need to move their families close to the mountain of gold and leave the band who still wanted to raid and kill.

The new leader was going to move the village to the land of the big lake to fight with Chief Winnemucca and rid their land of settlers. They had stolen many horses and killed many white men and they hoped to drive the white men out of the Pah Ute's land with one big raid.

White Bird had found a valley the man with the cows had not found, it had water and plenty of grass for their horses. The band was getting ready to move their camp to another place further to the west. White Bird had made ready to move but it would be in the other direction from their band. White Bird's wife, Fawn Skin, and Moon Glow had everything loaded on White Bird's horses ready to go to the new valley.

Moon Glow was loading one of the horses and the pack slipped and she fell down just as Tee was walking past. Tee helped her to her feet and they stood touching for a long time. Moon Glow's time of mourning was now finished and it would be up to her if they became one. Tee felt her back into him so he held her a little tighter. She turned and asked if he would like to share her bed and become one.

With all the packs loaded, White Bird started for their new home high in the mountains, just a short ride from the mountain with yellow rock. They rode into the mountains to the south and east of their camp. This valley was best entered from the east side of the mountains. The first night they camped at a small lake by a stream tumbling over the rocks to the lake. Moon Glow set up her own camp this night. Fawn Skin and she had been smiling at each other all day. When White Bird saw the two camps he started to speak but, with a hand raised, his wife gave him a smile and he knew.

Moon Glow's two children came over to ask if they could sleep with them tonight. With a hand she guided the two into their place to sleep. Tee was met by Moon Glow. They went to the stream to wash. She had found a pool behind their camp. Using some soap root, they washed each other and then walked back to camp. Tee now had two children and a wife and he was a happy man.

Tee and his new wife got up and headed back to the pool before any light was showing in the east. They had spent most of the night making love and talking. When they got into the pool they came together one more time. They finished washing when the sun was starting to light the sky behind the mountains. Walking back to camp, they were now a family looking forward to their new life.

Camp was loaded and the little band started moving to their new home. The two women were happy and the kids were throwing sticks and rocks along the way. White Bird was leading and Tee was staying back for protection from anyone following. They had been climbing most of the day and had just come over a pass leading into the valley below. White Bird was working his way down a small game trail through the trees. You could see the valley with the stream winding along in between the trees as they came down off the mountain.

White Bird had found this valley only a few years ago and had a camp site in mind as they reached the valley floor. The spot he wanted was backed up to a solid rock face reaching up to the sky. Water and firewood were close at hand, and the only way to reach this camp was directly from the front.

The small band was now alone with no one to help them if they had any problems. The two men went out to hunt and see if there was any sign of others having been in the valley. The two women went to work making the camp into a home for their men to come back to after a hunt. The two kids found many things to do as the women set up their lodges.

White Bird caught a movement ahead and stopped in his tracks, testing the wind. It was in his face so that was good. Tee had seen him stop so he crouched down slow so not to spook whatever White Bird had seen.

White Bird used a hand signal to bring Tee up behind him. Looking through the trees they could see a herd of elk feeding among the trees. They would need to move real slow stalking the elk herd.

Young bulls were a problem when trying to make a stalk. They like to run around all over the place. If one of these young bulls spots you the whole herd will spook.

The two men got down on their bellies and crawled forward inches at a time until they were in bow range. They needed to pick different animals and had to shoot at about the same time. Using sign language, they nocked the arrows on the string. Raising at the same time, they pulled back and released the arrows.

Nocking a second arrow, they were ready. One of the larger bulls spooked and ran right at them. Each of the men stepped behind a tree and let the bull come. As he passed they both released their arrows into the large bull and with a big crash the bull was down. Now they had to find the other two cows they had killed.

Walking forward to the location the cows had been when they released their arrows, they started looking for a blood trail. They found blood at both locations and started tracking the animals. Not over 50 yards from where they had been hit with the arrows, the cows were down. Tee started back to get the two horses and White Bird started cleaning and skinning the two cows. When Tee went past the large bull he stopped and opened him up, getting the guts out so the carcass could start to cool.

Before Tee started back with the horses he had used a rock and his knife to remove the ivory from the bull's teeth. He would keep one and give the other to White Bird. This would make a good present for their wives. With the two elk skinned and meat loaded on the horses, White Bird was ready to start back to the camp. Tee gave him the ivory to take to Moon Glow. Tee would stay and start skinning the big bull. This would be a big task. Working his knife around the knees then cutting down the inside of the leg, the hide started to come off. With the hide off all four legs he now started to cut along the belly pulling the hide back. He would try to get the hide loose on one side down to the backbone. This way he could roll the elk over and do the other side.

Elk hide is hard to cut but he had it almost done when he heard White Bird coming back with the horses. Now he had some help to cut off the legs and head and start packing the meat back to camp.

Tying the quarters together, they placed one on each side of the horses. They had cut out the back strap and it was inside of the skin. The two men sat down and started cutting up the heart, eating it raw. They now headed back to camp to start smoking the meat. The smoking would take a few days to finish. The weather was cold now so the meat would not spoil.

My friend Sandy talking about Ronnie and Abby along the river

Chapter 22 ABBY GETS A RING

Ronnie was riding over the Sierras from time to time depending on who was sick or went off to some other job. Bolivar figured the gold mines got some of them where they could make better money and not have to fight the Indians. On one trip Ronnie was getting some supplies at a store near Sacramento when he saw some rings in a box on the counter.

The owner of the store told Ronnie he had purchased the rings and other stuff from travelers that needed supplies and were short on cash. Ronnie found a set of rings and paid cash for them.

Fall was coming on and Ronnie wanted to make it over to Buckland to see Abby again soon. He was thinking about some more of that kissing and maybe even some other stuff, if things worked out.

Ronnie had been thinking if Abby would like to marry him and move to his ranch. A nice ring may be just the thing to have when he asked her. He was supposed to ride back to Carson City during the next week. He would be covering some days off for the other riders.

When he got back he was going to ask Bolivar for a week off to visit Buckland Station. He told him he wanted to talk to a friend. No one knew about Abby, or his large ranch in Eastern Nevada.

If Abby would marry him he would ride until the spring or mid summer depending on how things went at Buckland Station. That would be 1861 and he would have turned seventeen by then. Abby would be seventeen in May so that would be a great time to head to the ranch if she would be willing.

His mom never had a ring that nice. He hadn't been able to find her rings after the fire. Over the next week he worked back over to Carson City. At breakfast the next morning Bolivar came in.

Ronnie said, "I need a week to visit Buckland Station, if you need any horses moved over that way I will take them when I go.

Bolivar said, "we will need some mules over there next month, but you could take them with you when you go."

I said, "Could you have the mules ready in the morning? If so I will head out then. If Lighting or Buster is in the barn, can I take one of them?"

"Sure, go ahead, you just make sure you don't take any more money from the Army boys this trip," he chuckled.

"How did you hear about that?"

"Well, Pony Bob liked to fall off a chair telling about how he set you up for the race and made you put up the money. The best part was that he got half. He still thinks that was great fun."

With the sun coming up I headed east with my mule pack train. After a bit the mules came along at a fine pace. It would be late getting into Buckland. I had a few ideas I wanted to talk to Abbey about. When you have a ring in your pocket and kissing on your mind, you do come up with some fine ideas. Having those ideas sometimes make it a little hard to get settled in the saddle.

After dropping the mules at Fort Churchill, I made a short trip on over to Buckland. I thought I would just walk in and order dinner to surprise Abby but she had seen me come in and was walking out to the corrals by the time I stripped the gear off Lighting. When I reached the gate we both figured it was time to get started and we did, I do think we about have the kissing part down real good and getting better all the time.

Abby said she wanted to show me some place I would like. She took my hand and led me to her wagon. When we got to the wagon she said, "pull back the flap and let's climb up, I have a trunk we can sit on at the head of the bed." With the back cover pulled back in place, we were alone. Abby reach back and lit a lantern as it was getting dark.

Abby said, "This was Mom and Dad's bed. We could talk and kiss a little bit if you want." The next thing I knew we were laying on our sides facing each other and she was in my arms. We had been kissing a while and I was having that problem again, I put my hands on her face and said, "Abby I need to ask you something."

"Look, I hope you like me as much as I like you because, I want to get married. I got a ring in California and I hope you will say yes. Ronnie pulled out the ring and Abby went stiff and asked how did you get that ring?

"I got it in California at a trading post." She was crying hard now and I did not know what to do! "Abby, what is wrong? "She just kept crying and crying. After a bit, her sobs started to lessen. All I could do was lay there and hold her until she calmed down so we could talk about it.

"Ronnie this ring was my mother's! I forgot to get it off her hand before they buried her in Utah." She kissed me then like I had never been kissed. I was on fire, after a bit she pulled back and said. "Yes! I will be proud to marry you." We were laying there together and I was thinking if this being married got any better I didn't think I could stand it.

After a while Abby said "I would like to love you all the way but I want to be pure when we get married. Is that ok?"

I said, "It may be better if I let you go back to your room and maybe I could sleep here."

Abby said she would like to keep this bed special, but her bed was up front and I could use that one.

I said "Ok, I will be thinking about you all night when I am sleeping in your bed. That will be much better than the hay mow in the barn.

With the light burning low, Ronnie laid down in Abby's bed. After a while he reached over and turned the wick down on the lantern and he went to sleep - dreaming of her all night.

During the next few days they kept away from the bed in the wagon and talked about everything, including how long Ronnie was going to ride for the Pony Express. Ronnie felt that if he rode over the winter and into May they would have good grass for the horses to make the trip home to their ranch. It was all set. They would see each other when they could and would get married at Buckland Station on May 9th 1861. Then they would start the trip back to their ranch and home.

*

The winter of 1860 started off with a bang, Ronnie was riding from Carson City west into the Sierras. The weather had put long coats on all of the horses and the crisp air added some punch to their steps. A light snow was falling as Ronnie rode out with the mail. His horse had given a few crow hops when he started to gallop.

The first part of his ride would only have a small climb, but when he reached Mormon Station the snow flakes were falling fast. It was a wet snow and was sticking to the trees and bushes. The exchange was good at Mormon Station and his new horse was fast. Ronnie had used him before when doing relief riding during the summer and fall.

Ronnie was glad to be able to only carry his pistol now that winter weather starting and the trouble with the Indians was over. He kept the extra two cylinders ready on his belt if needed though. He would be taking the new route today. In the past he would have gone on to Woodfords Station but today he would start the climb up to Friday's Station.

He would climb over 3,000 feet right up the face of the Sierras and over the top and then down to the lake. By the time Ronnie got to the base of the mountain it had been snowing for a few hours at this higher elevation. The trail was hard to follow due to the snow. He had never been over this route before. The next problem was his horse was used to the old trail. When he left Mormon Station the horse had wanted to take the old trail.

Now it was getting colder by the minute. The snow was piling up on the trail but Ronnie could still see some spots of it. When he climbed into the pines things was a little better, he could see most of the trail in among the trees. He had to give it to this horse, he could climb. After a bit he pulled him to a stop to let him blow. This guy just pulled at the bit and wanted to get to the next station.

Ronnie had been one of the fastest riders but this ride would not be one of them. When Ronnie was eating breakfast today he had spent some time talking with one of the men who had cut the trail leading up to Friday's Station. Ronnie was thinking back on what Andy Sams had said about this new trail. Andy talked about some key marks and how the trail worked its way up the mountain.

He was at one of the key points now, thinking back to what Andy had said. I make a swing to the left leading into a canyon. When you reach the far side, look for a dead fall snag on the side of the canyon. You will find the trail leading up to the ridge. When you reach the ridge, stay on the spine for about a mile, then you will drop down a little to a saddle. Slide off the right side of the saddle. You will find the trail running between two large rocks.

Ronnie had lost the trail in the saddle and had to cut back and forth in the timber until he found the two rocks. Back on the trail again, he would need to now follow the side of the mountain until he came to another flat section with timber.

Andy had said to go straight across this flat and re-enter the timber on the other side. You will find a pine tree with a blazed mark on it. Andy had cut this blaze with an axe. To be sure you are on the right trail, look back when you leave the timber and you will see the same mark on the tree leading back onto the trail heading east.

Ronnie would need to keep in the trees for about two miles until he came to a small stream. When he reached the stream he pulled his horse in to let him have a drink. Ronnie stepped down and got a drink of the ice cold water just upstream from his horse. Stepping back up, he now had to find the trail off the back side of this mountain. His next mark would be a large bolder with a flat side, the trail would head down just past it on the flat side.

This horse was a good mountain breed and was sure footed. He came down the trail with snow and ice with no problem. On some of the drops his horse was sliding his hind feet and easing down with only his front. When Ronnie got off this mountain he felt like he had been chased by a hundred Indians. He was tired. Friday's Station came into sight from the ridge. The last few miles would not be a problem if they did not step into a hole covered by snow. Ronnie headed down off the ridge trying to keep on the trail. Some parts of the trail had been uncovered by the wind.

Ronnie had made it without any major problems. He pulled into Fridays Station at a trot. His horse was ready for some food and oats and Ronnie was looking for a stove and some food also. Making the exchange to the new rider, he walked his horse back to the stable. The horse handler took his horse back to strip off the saddle and give him a good rubdown.

When it was his time to make the return trip with the mail it was going to be dark with only a little moon. The best part of this was the trail would show hoof prints along the trail. Ronnie was waiting for the mail with the horse he had ridden up from Mormon Station, so they knew each other and both had been over the trail once.

With the mochila in place, he was off at a gallop. Snow was flying from the horse's hooves as he rode down the trail. This mountain bred horse was good and sure footed. He just seemed to remember the way. When he started up the trail leading to the first ridge, this horse stayed at a trot all the way up. Once on top he just kept moving along the trail. He seemed to know every twist & turn to make it back to Mormon Station.

Ronnie just gave him his head and this horse never slowed down. When they came to the stream he stopped and took a few sips and off they went along the mountain and into the trees by the flat sided rock. Riding along the spine of the mountain was a thrill in the dark with ice and snow on the trail.

When Ronnie came off the canyon wall and past the snag, he knew he was making time. He dropped off the ridge leading down to the flat among the trees. It was so dark he couldn't see much. Suddenly he saw a light from Mormon Station out in front of him and a new horse was waiting.

Mochila passed and he was up heading to Carson Station at a gallop. He stayed at a gallop for a few miles then this new horse dropped to a ground eating trot. This new horse knew the way and he never moved off the trail. Ronnie thought "this guy could trot all day without a rest."

He watched the geese down in the river. They must be some that never leave the local area during the winter. The snow was gone at this lower elevation and it was good not to have to worry about the horse falling on the ice.

Carson Station was coming into sight and he could see the next horse ready to go, it was Buster. He pulled off the mochila and put it on Buster. Walking around in front he gave him a rub on his nose. He pushed back and wanted more but the next rider was up. McPherson was going down the trail heading east. Ronnie was headed to the bunk house for some sleep.

When he got up the next day he looked at the ride roster and found out he was to head east to Fort Churchill later that day. He would get to see Abby and get in a little kissing and some other stuff!

Sitting at the table eating, Andy came in to talk. He had been shoeing a horse. Andy wanted to know how the new trail worked out. He and another guy had cleared the trail with mules only a few weeks ago. Ronnie told him he had made it ok but it was due to the horse and not him.

Ronnie had time for a short nap before he was due to head east with the mail. Lying in his bunk he got to thinking about Abby and getting married in a few months. His life was going to change. They would be heading back to the ranch as a married couple. He wanted to see Diamond and start working with his colts too.

He got up and grabbed a couple of biscuits and put them in his pocket for later, a snack is always good along the trail. He walked out to find Lighting waiting and he wanted some rubs.

This would be a fast ride heading east to Fort Churchill and Abby. The rider came in and Ronnie put the mochila on Lighting and they were off at full speed. Ronnie let him run for about two miles then eased him back to a fast trot, thinking he would keep this pace up all the way. The trail was muddy most of the way so it was nice when they got along the river in the sand.

Lightning set a record for the run from Carson City to Dayton Station. The next exchanges on the way to Fort Churchill were all good. After making the last exchange at Fort Churchill, Ronnie walked his last horse back for a good rubdown. He told the horse handler to take some time off and he would take care of this horse. After settling Lightning in he asked the station manager if he could use one of the other horses as he needed to go over to Buckland Station for a while.

When he reached Buckland he walked in to get a bite to eat. He had heated some water and had washed off some of the trail dirt from his trip. Abby was surprised to see him. They talked as he ate and made plans to spend the evening in her wagon.

Abby climbed into the wagon and joined him on the bed in the front of the wagon.

After kissing for a while Ronnie started rubbing her breasts through her dress and after a bit started to unbutton her dress front. Her nipples were hard as a rock under his hand. Abby held his hand to her breasts for a while then said we had better slow down some.

Ronnie would be riding back to Carson City in the morning so they just lay holding each other talking and kissing some. It was getting late when Abby got up and re-buttoned her dress and walked back to her bed.

Ronnie got up and went to his horse and rode back to Fort Churchill to get ready to ride back to Carson City.

Most of the winter Ronnie rode over the Sierras, and into California keeping the mail moving forward. Bolivar was having problems keeping riders. The winter was cold with lots of snow and at times Bolivar had Andy and a crew taking mules over the trail to keep it open. Bolivar also used the mules to help Warren Upson to get the mail over Echo Summit a few times during the winter. For a short time Bolivar had Ronnie working his way west as a relief rider. Twice during the winter he got over to Sacramento then worked his way back to Carson.

Chapter 23 RONNIE GETS A BRIDE

The last week in April, Ronnie made a mail run to Carson from Fort Churchill. When he was ready to start back, he picked up one of the Standard-bred geldings of Abby's so when he quit in the first week in May he would have a horse to ride back to Buckland Station.

May 9th came and the weather was great. Ronnie met with the preacher and his wife. They had a covered wagon and drove from town to town preaching the word of God to all that would listen. Abby had made a dress and Ronnie had a new outfit just for the wedding.

When the service was about ready, all of the people from Buckland Station came and Pony Bob rode in just in time.

Bob said, "you can't do this alone, but my problem is, how do I get more spending money from horse racing with you gone back east some place. By the way, why do you want to go back east anyway?"

Ronnie said, "I have a small ranch east of here and that is where we are going to live."

With the wedding over and the bride kissed, and all the good wishes over. Ronnie hitched the team and tied off the other horses to the wagon. They headed down the wagon road headed east not west. It seemed as if everyone else was headed west. Abby was on the seat waiting for Ronnie to climb up when Pony Bob called out. He was going down the trail with Buster, running flat out.

Ronnie slapped the rains down and they headed across the Carson River, Abby slid over next to Ronnie and kissed him on the cheek. She leaned over and said "lets not go too far tonight. We have some things to do tonight if you want."

They drove east for a couple of hours and Ronnie had a spot planned for their first night. It was off the trail about a mile and he would be able to swing back on to the trail heading east with little trouble.

Ronnie went to work getting the horses on some grass and hauled water to them. He was ready to go to the wagon and get into bed with Abby for the first time. He was a little scared. This was new to him and he knew she had never been with a man either, so how was this going to work.

Ronnie stepped up on the back of the wagon and opened the flap. Abby said, “take your clothes off and come to bed.” Ronnie sat on the back gate of the wagon thinking. How do I do this without falling out of the back of the wagon? When he got down to his long johns he was sweating and short of breath. He had never been alone with any women before and was hard as a rock.

Then Abby said “the long johns too.” The lamp was turned low and when he reached down to pull back the covers he could just see that she was naked. Ronnie looked at her and said, “ooh my God, Abby, we are going make this work.” Abby reached up and took his hand pulling him down beside her on their bed. Still holding his hand she placed it on her breast and he could feel her nipples harden and pucker. Ronnie reached between her legs and touched her. She was ready. He kissed her and said you do know this is going to hurt the first time. “Abby pulled him over her and smiled, reaching between them she guided him to her.

Later they lay spent in each others arms. Abby said, “we did just great, right? You could never know how much I love you.”

Ronnie said, “I think I love you more, and thank you for being my wife and lover.”

They lay facing each other until they both went to sleep feeling that this first time could not have been any better.

The light was just starting to show in the east when she woke. Abby could hardly believe she was in her man’s arms. Laying there, she thought about having her way with him. This time would be fun. She took him in her hand and felt him harden, then raised up over him taking him just a little at a time and when she finished she said, “you do know I am the boss, right?”.

Ronnie said, "you can be the boss any time you want." After enjoying each other in the soft light of morning, Ronnie got dressed and went out to get the fire going. When the water was hot, Ronnie took a pail of warm water to the wagon so Abigail could wash up and get ready for the day.

This was the first day of their life together and it was going to be filled with many new and exciting things. They had weeks to get to the ranch and no time schedule to keep.

Ronnie wanted to show Abby a special place he had found when riding for the Pony Express. He had ridden upstream from the trail one day to check out the stream. After a short ride he found a large pool of water and it was deep and clear.

With time on their hands, he felt it would be a great place to camp on the way to Spring Creek. Ronnie and Abby were just getting to know each other so a bath in the river might be nice.

Ronnie was driving the team and Abby had been reaching over and touching him and smiling. He turned to her and said, "in about an hour we will be pulling into our campsite and it will be my turn to do some touching."

Abby just gave him a big smile and let her hand linger a little longer. This was driving him nuts. Ronnie pulled the team in among the cottonwoods by the stream. He got the horses on a picket line and got a fire started. Turning and taking Abby's hand, he led her upstream and stopped at the pool.

Now he said "Let's get out of our clothes and jump in." With clothes on the bank, the two jumped into the water naked. Abby tried to get away but Ronnie caught her in seconds. Yes, it was his turn to do some touching. When he turned her around to face him she wrapped her legs around him and they came together.

They stayed together just enjoying each other. When finished they spent an hour washing each other and talking. Neither was in any hurry to go back to camp and fix dinner.

The next day they reached Spring Creek and stopped to stay and enjoy the country. They saw some of the Pony Express Riders from time to time but they were at the point where they were about ready to leave the trail and head a little north, leaving that part of their life behind.

Ronnie was looking forward to seeing Mr. Brown and showing off Abby to him. He was sure that Juanita and Abby would be great company for each other. It was good to be headed back to the ranch now to see how much work had been finished.

When they made camp that night, Ronnie got the stock out on grass and water. He came in to check on dinner. Abby had that well in hand so he got a cup of coffee and sat down on the wagon tongue to drink it. Abby came over and had a seat beside him and they talked about the day.

Ronnie turned to Abby and said "you do know I have some gold don't you?"

She answered, "I have a feeling you have more than you let on."

Ronnie said, "we have a lot of gold. In fact we are rich; we have more gold than we could spend. You need to know that we can't talk about it to anyone at anytime though. When we get back, we will go out and camp for a week at a stream so I can pan out another few bags. We will take this wagon and camp like we are now. We will tell Juan and Juanita we just want to spend some time alone. After we get a few more sacks we will need to take a trip to California to put most of it in a bank in Sacramento."

Ronnie went on to explain that Pa told him about how people would change if they knew about the gold. Ronnie was afraid even Juan and Juanita would change if they knew. So he warned Abby to not say a word about it to anyone. Abby asked about going to Sacramento. Would they ride the horses or take the wagon?

Ronnie said they would take the horses to Mr. Brown's store and have him keep them for us. Then they would take the stagecoach over to California. However, if they got much more gold, they would ride over and camp along the way. Abby got up and moved over to the fire to finish their dinner, Ronnie just kept looking at his wife, thinking just how lucky he was in so many ways.

After they had dinner Abby pulled him over and wrapped her arms around his neck. With her face about an inch from his, she told him that she still couldn't believe he had found her mother's rings and given them to her. "Many times each day, I just turn the rings around my finger and remember my mother. They mean so much to me. I think we need to go to bed so I can thank you proper like." She had thought her mother's rings were lost forever. Now Abby started to have bad feelings about Bob Stanton and Joe Harding because they had stolen the rings. Someday they would meet again.

Abigail was driving the team when they pulled into Mr. Brown's Store. Ronnie was riding one of the Standard-bred geldings. Ronnie came back to the wagon and helped Abby down. Mr. Brown came out asking, "well just who is this, Ronnie?"

"This is my wife Abigail Campbell, we met over at Buckland Station and here we are."

After greetings were exchanged they went into the store. Ronnie asked how Juan was doing and how much money did he owe for supplies.

Mr. Brown answered "I got to tell you when you got that pair you picked a couple of winners. Juanita is trading me eggs and clay pots for about everything they need, and Juan has taken six of my horses and topped them off for me. So to tell you the truth we are just about even from when you left. What do you need to take with you? You still have some credit." Abby picked up some extra blankets and other stuff to restock the wagon. When she finished, Mr. Brown said, "Let me feed you tonight. It is getting too late to start today anyway. Besides, I would like to hear about your time out west. Did you ever get over to California?" They talked until late that night and had a great time. When Ronnie and Abby headed back to the wagon, Mr. Brown told them that the cook would have breakfast ready at first light so just to come on in and eat."

The sun was peeking over the hills as they started to the ranch. It would still take a couple of days yet, but they were almost home. When they stopped to eat some lunch and let the horses graze, Ronnie went to find Abby. W hen he lifted the back flap on the wagon she was waiting for him, laying on the bed.

When they got back on the trail heading to the ranch, Ronnie told Abby about Mr. & Mrs. Applegate and their ranch. They should be getting there tomorrow some time in the afternoon. He told her about when they took him in and taught him about ranching, horses, and cattle things.

The next day they started to pull into a large wash when Ronnie told Abby about when Juan had his horse killed and he saved the day. Ronnie told her how he almost had not gone after the Indians but sure was glad he had. He pointed to a spot down the wash and told her that was where Juan had been trapped under his horse and would have been killed.

"You should have seen the Indians when I rode up from behind and shot the one with the rifle. I then emptied the Spencer at the Indians and they thought I was out of shells. Well, they figured wrong, I had the Henry out of the boot when I came over the edge of the wash. The Indians found themselves looking down the barrel of that Henry with fifteen rounds, I killed two more and the last Indian was headed home as fast as his horse would run."

Later that day, Little John came riding up to see who was coming to visit the ranch. When he saw who it was he let out a yell and came in at a canter, "Ronnie how are you doing, and who is this, did she get lost or what?"

"No, this is my wife and we are coming home to the ranch."

Little John said "I will go on ahead and tell Mom and Dad you are heading home and will be stopping by." When they reached the ranch house Sam and Beth were both waiting on the porch. Sam helped Abby down and when her feet hit the ground Beth said "Welcome! Come on in so we can talk while I get dinner on the table."

Abby jumped in and helped finish up with the food and set the table. Beth was so happy to have someone to talk to she never quit chattering until dinner was on the table.

Beth called out to the men to wash up before the food gets cold. Dinner was a great time. Sam told Ronnie how much he was helped by selling the horses to the Pony Express at such a high price. You will never know how much that helped to get us on top.

Ronnie said, "Sam, after dinner we need to talk some about horses." With the women putting up dinner the men went out on to the porch to talk. Ronnie told Sam about the big stud of Abby's and her mares. "Look Sam, I have an idea. I had the stud cover all of her mares so they all should be in foal. Why don't I leave the stallion with you to cover your mare. Then you can bring him up to the ranch when he gets his job done.

Sam said, "That should make him happy and it sure would help me out. I would like to get another team ready in a few years."

Sam continued, "Ronnie, you should have some yearlings if Diamond did his job.

"Yeah, I can't wait to see what I have."

Sam said, "Man, that Juan and Juanita are the best. They stop by on their way to the store and from what I hear, they have a nice house and the barn is about finished.

"Tony came by with that Palomino a few days back.. What a horse he is. I would like to get him to breed a couple of my mares. I still can't believe that guy was going to kill you and Tony for the horses. Son, you have come a long way. If you hadn't been ready, you and Tony would have both been dead."

In the morning, with good byes said, they started down the road with the stallion staying to do his job. He was talking to his mares for as long as they could hear. Abby said she thought that he was telling his mares that he had a new girl.

That afternoon they camped by a small stream Ronnie knew about. While it was still daylight they went to a pool up a ways from camp. They had a great time washing each other and talking about what they wanted to do with the ranch. In the morning Ronnie told her they could be getting to the ranch by late afternoon. Ronnie had the team hitched and Abby got out some meat left over from their dinner so they could eat on the road today.

When he climbed up on the seat and started the team, Abby gave him a sandwich to eat. She took the lines and drove on toward home, her new home. Noon was a short stop just to rest the team and then back on the road to the ranch. Ronnie was pushing a little because he wanted to get in before dark.

The sun was just sliding down behind the hills when they pulled into the ranch yard. By the time they got the team pulled up everyone was talking. Abby fell in love with Juanita and the kids, Tony was just great also. Abby and Juanita fixed dinner and Juan and Tony filled Ronnie in on the progress they had made.

Then and only then when the food was on the table did the talk slow down. Juanita asked for quiet so she could tell about the palomino Ronnie and Tony got from the killer. She told about her family having a big rancho outside of Sacramento, California and how her brother had raised that horse from a baby.

Ronnie and Abby just sat there and listened to the story never having thought Juanita was from an aristocratic family. Ronnie asked if she was sure about the horse. It was then that she told of Victor's name on the underside of the saddle. Juanita was crying now with Juan holding her, after a bit she turned to Ronnie and asked if she and Juan could travel to Sacramento to see her family.

Juan went on to tell about how they had run away to get married because her family did not approve of him. Victor was the only one who liked him, but both of her parents had wanted better for her. Ronnie asked, "how could they not like a man that was half owner of a twenty thousand acre ranch?"

Juan and Juanita both stood up and asked, "what did you say?"

Ronnie told them the second time that they were half owners of this ranch.

"When did this happen" they asked.

Ronnie gave them a little smile, "when we got the cattle back to the ranch and then I went to ride the Pony Express. I sent in the papers just in case I was killed. Was this a good time to tell you or would you have liked me to wait?"

Juan was shaking his hand and Juanita was hugging him as hard as she could, they both said, "We would have never guessed, we were just happy to have a place to live and raise the kids.

'OK now, Juanita, back to your question about going to California, why don't Abby and I go with you two and that will be our wedding trip." Ronnie said. "Tony is that ok with you. We need you to stay on and look after things during the time we are away."

Tony said, "Si, of course, that is good for me."

Ronnie told everyone that they would stay at the ranch for a day or two and then he wanted to take Abby to a spot he was thinking about building a house. The place is back in the hills a few miles from here, the little valley has timber and good water. I like it real well and want to show it to Abby before starting to build our home.

Then he asked Juan "how did Diamond do with the mares?"

"Well, they all dropped some great looking foals. I have been handling them some. I built a corral back there in one of the little draws, and every week or so I take grain to feed them. By the time I get in the corral they are all in there with me ready for their treat. All but one are fillies. The little stud colt looks just like Diamond and he likes to run all the time, he never seems to stop."

Ronnie said, "Tony, what are you going to do with that Palomino stud?"

"Well, I would like to get some mares of my own and raise some horses I am partial to his color."

Ronnie asked Juanita if there were any other ranches that had Palominos that she knew of. She said that one of her girlfriend's father raised them also. When we get over to California we may be able to purchase some mares from him. It was late when they all went to bed but planned to be up at first light to look over the horse herd.

The sun was starting to show in the east when they were sitting at the table having breakfast and talking about the day. Tony said they should be ready for a fight any time because he had seen some unshod pony tracks in the back country during the last week.

Juan got out the extra guns and checked all of the loads and placed extra rounds close at hand. When the men rode out they all had their Henrys loaded and ready.

Juan led the way back into the hills to the series of valleys where he had the horses grazing. When he came to the pole fence he stopped to open the gate so they could all ride in. With the gate closed he mounted and started off at a lope. After about thirty minutes they spotted the horses. Juan led the way to the corral he had made and when they rode in the horses followed, Juan had the grain ready when they all got there.

Diamond came right up to Ronnie, wanting a good rub. After giving him some grain he went to look over the other horses. He was able to handle all of the little ones. The little stud was quite active and was running around everywhere.

Ronnie asked Juan when he wanted to wean them off the mares.

"I have enough grass cut to hold them at the ranch house until next spring." Juan answered. "Tony can start working with them while we are gone if you like."

"Ok, let's get a rope on them and bring them along when we head home."

Ronnie was looking up along the stream and said that we missed one of the horses.

"No" Juan said, "we have them all in the pen."

Well there is another horse along the stream, lets go and take a look see." When they got there they found the horse of Tony's that he had given to the Indian that had been hurt. Well damn, look at that! Who would have ever thought they would see that horse again?

After a bit Ronnie pulled out his Henry and told the others to get armed. Out of the trees came the Indian that had been hurt, the one they called White Bird. As he came he held up both arms showing he was not armed. Ronnie put back the Henry and started to ride out to meet him. Ronnie noticed he had six mares with him. When they got close the Indian got down and waited for Ronnie to ride up to him.

It was about lunch time so Ronnie had Tony pick up some wood for a fire and put on a pot of coffee. The girls had packed some meat and bread for their lunch so they put out the food and Ronnie pointed to the Indian to come over and eat with them.

In a bit the Indian came over and picked up some meat and bread. The coffee wasn't anything he had ever drank before, but took a cup and worked on it some.

When they finished eating, the Indian motioned for Ronnie to come over and look at his mares and then pointed to Diamond and back to his mares. After a bit they figured he wanted Diamond to breed his mares. Ronnie gave him a head nod and pointed to the mares and to the stud and then closed his hands. The White Bird had a big smile and went over to turn his mares loose. Diamond would do his job when the time was right.

Juan said, "He had to make those tracks I saw last week. He was waiting for us to check the horses. Tony went over to the gelding and led it back to White Bird and handed him the rope. Tony was talking to him and telling him that he had given him the horse. The Indian couldn't understand at first, but he figured it out and took the rope.

Tony looked over to Ronnie and Juan and said, "we may need a friend some time." They agreed and said, "not a bad idea but you know that my dad was killed by this band of Indians, don't you? But this is a new time and we could use a friendly Indian in the tribe."

With lunch finished, they got ready to ride out back to the ranch. Ronnie turned back to the Indian and pointed to the fire and took a stick and drew a teepee and pointed to the Indian. He got the idea and got his bed roll and laid it out beside the fire. Ronnie said "well boys, lets hope we have a friend. Diamond will make sure he has some good horses next year.

Chapter 24 EXPANDING THE BANK

After a few days Ronnie and Abby started out to the little valley they had talked about to find a spot to build their new home. Ronnie had told Juan they would be gone for a couple of weeks.

"If we find a place to build our home we may come back sooner but don't bother to follow us unless there is a need. Abby and I are going to explore the valleys in that area. I have never taken a good look so now is the time to do just that."

"Abby, we should be there about dark or there about." Ronnie was right-it was dark when he stopped alongside a small stream and started to unhitch the team.

Abby got out the lanterns and started to cook some dinner and make the coffee. With dinner on his plate and a cup of coffee in his hand, Ronnie turned to Abby and said, "when we leave here we will be rich and I do mean rich."

Abby turned to Ronnie and said, "come with me. I want to show you something, I want you to look at what my Mom and Dad left me."

Climbing into the wagon and over the front seat Ronnie asked, "are you thinking about what I am?"

"No, this is serious! Well, I think that is serious also, but look here and pull out that little nail, now slide the cover off the back of the seat."

"My God, Abby! That is full of money!"

"I just wanted you to know that I came to you with a little money of my own." Abby said. "We need to count it. I have never even looked at this money. I figured with all the money you had we may want to put this into a bank also."

Ronnie said, "I can't believe you never said anything about this cash."

"Like I said, I never knew how much Mom and Dad sold the store and house for." After counting the cash and coins they had another five thousand dollars.

"I can't believe you never looked to see what was in the safe box. Now you are rich. Does a rich girl want to help finish what I was thinking about a little while ago?

"Well, Mr. Rich Man, lets see who can get under the covers first gets to be the boss." Abby shucked her stuff first and then she showed him that she was still the boss.

After a while Ronnie said "I didn't want to say anything, but this stream is full of gold. You know, when I told you we was rich I still don't know just how much gold we have. When we head to California I want to have another couple of bags to take with us. If it's ok, we can use your cash to cover expenses on the trip. Now we can just keep quiet about the gold."

"What we need to do is, during the day I will pan for gold and you will keep watch. We can't have anyone know about this. I would like to have two more sacks of gold along with what I have in the wagon." Then Ronnie said, "I have another idea and I want you to let me know what you think about it. What do you think if we rode over to California instead of taking the stage?"

Abby said, "That would be fun. Also, you must be thinking that we could hide the gold better with a couple of pack horses. Am I right?"

Ronnie said, "You have the idea. We could let Juan and Juanita take the stage and by the time we get there they would have had time to sort things out with her family.

The two weeks went fast and Ronnie was starting to find less gold each day, but he had his two bags and was ready to start back.

Abby was out walking and went up a side stream for a ways. She stopped for a rest and happened to look behind her at the rock wall. It was a vertical wall, about twenty feet tall. The sun was just right and she saw a little flash. She got up to get a better look.

It was broken quartz with gold in it. This was what Ronnie and his dad had been looking for all along. Abby headed back to camp to tell Ronnie. When she got there, she looked at Ronnie and said "do you know how much gold we have?"

He said, "Well yeah", we have the four bags now and what you have in the bank, right?"

Abby smiled and took his hand and led him back to the rock face with the broken quartz and said, "well we now have a lot more. We are now even richer than what you thought."

Ronnie said, "Stay here. I am going to get a pick and take a better look. I will be right back." With the pick Ronnie broke out some of the rock and crushed it with the side of the pick's blade. He found nuggets and fine gold flakes. This must be where the stream got the gold that I found. Yes, Abby, we are rich, in fact real rich.

Abby said, "what are we going to do with all of this money?"

"We will come back from time to time and mine it and make trips to different places to put it in a bank." Ronnie told her. Pa said not to ever put gold in any bank more than once. If you do, they will talk and then things go bad. That is why we need to keep quiet about this. We will only spend a little at a time unless we have a reason to do otherwise."

When they went to bed that night Abby told Ronnie she wanted to make love like rich folks. Ronnie then asked, "how is that done, may I ask?".

Abby told him to start with a little kiss and then we will see how it ends up. Later, laying in each others arms, Ronnie said, "I think being rich and in love will do quite nicely". They slept in until the sun was up. It would only be a short trip back to the ranch. They could make it by dark even with the late start.

Chapter 25 GETTING HOME TO THE RANCH

They pulled into the ranch as the sun was setting behind the mountains to the west. Juanita had dinner ready with enough for all. Tony had returned from the store and had brought along the big stud, he had done his job. Sam had sent the stud home with many thanks.

At dinner Ronnie and Abby told of their change of plans about having Juan and Juanita go on ahead of them on the stagecoach. Juanita was ready to head out in the morning but she had to get little Juan and Hector ready to travel.

Ronnie asked Juan to take the other wagon and team and leave them at Mr. Brown's store, and tell him he could use it to make deliveries if needed. Abby and I will follow in a few days, Ronnie went out to the wagon to get enough money to give Juan to cover their trip and the stagecoach fare to California and back.

Ronnie told Juan to take his Henry along with his Navy Colt pistol and load up the two extra cylinders in case he might need it. Then he told Juanita to do the same and keep the guns in a bag inside the coach. Keep the Henry with you all of the time and keep extra shells in the coach with you also. There have been hold ups on some of the stagecoaches in the past and having that Henry might make the difference.

The next day the men rode out to check on the horses to see if there had been any problems. When they got there all of the horses were ready to eat the grain they had brought. Ronnie rode over to the camp site to check it out. From what he could tell the Indian had stayed for about a week or two and had been gone just a day or so.

Ronnie rode back and told Juan and Tony the Indian had gone home. They hoped he was a happy Indian. Getting back, they found Juanita had the kids put to bed in the back of the wagon ready to start at first light. It would take a couple of days to make it to Mr. Brown's store so they wanted an early start. Little Juan and Hector could sleep later this way. With the sun coming up, they started to California to see if Juanita's family was ok after losing Victor. Ronnie told Tony to ride over to the Applegate place and see if Little John would like to work until they got back. In case he did, Ronnie gave Tony some money to pay him at the end of each week. Ronnie was sure Little John could use some extra spending money, knowing Sam was short of cash.

Ronnie and Abby got started the next day riding the two Standard bred geldings leading two pack horses. Ronnie had split the gold between the two pack horses with only a little in his saddle bags.

Both Ronnie and Abby had plenty of cash in their saddle bags to cover anything they needed on the trail to Sacramento. The weather was great. They hoped for a good ride to California and fun camping along the way. Ronnie was planning to make some stops in the mountains to show Abby some of the great views in the Sierra's. They might even get a chance to talk to Snowshoe Johnson when they got over to the other side of the Sierras.

Ronnie had talked to him a couple of times, but could never see how he could make the trips over the Sierra carrying about 100 pounds of mail in the snow. That was a real man if there was ever was one.

When they got to the store, Mr. Brown was glad to see them and said Juan and Juanita and the kids were on their way. Mr. Brown said Juan had told him he could use the team and wagon if he liked. He just wanted to confirm that with Ronnie.

Ronnie said, "Look, I will tell you now that Juan is my partner and whatever he said is good with me. While I'm here, I'd better get paid up, how much do I owe you?"

"Let's go in and see. I think about one hundred or so. I will take off some for using the team if that's ok with you," said Mr. Brown.

Ronnie answered, "Just figure the price and I will pay you."

After settling up and adding two hundred rounds of .44s for the Henry, Ronnie and Abby started for Spring Creek Station and then on west to Buckland Station. They planned on staying for a few days at Buckland Station so they could visit a bit before heading on to Carson City.

Ronnie hoped to see Bolivar Roberts in Carson City to see how things were going. One reason Ronnie quit was he had gotten the feeling the Pony Express was not going to be in operation by late summer. The telegraph lines were moving west fast and when they linked up to Sacramento the Pony Express would no longer be needed.

When they got into Spring Creek Ronnie asked around about if there had been any problems to the west. The report was only a robbery attempt once in a while. When the Pony Express rider came in heading east he told of a shoot out with one of the stagecoaches a few days ago.

Ronnie asked what had happened and the rider told him a young Mexican passenger had shot and killed two robbers and wounded another but that no one on the stage had been hurt. Ronnie turned to Abby and said, "that had to be Juan. He must have had that Henry talking loud and clear."

After getting the news, they started down the trail heading west. Ronnie said "we will camp at that stream where we camped before on the way to the ranch. Do you think the swimming hole is still there waiting for us? We had a good time there the last time if you remember. We just may need to take a bath. We have been on the road for a few days and the water sounds great."

"Lets ride!" Abby said.

After they set up camp that afternoon, they walked upstream and found the big hole was waiting just as before. Getting out of their clothes, they jumped in. The water felt wonderful. Ronnie washed Abby's hair and after a few dunks they climbed out onto the bank and dried off. Changing into clean duds, they went back to camp to finish cooking dinner. Coffee was ready in no time and tasted good. Ronnie took a cup and went outside of camp a ways to take in the sounds of the night. That is when he heard a voice coming from the west.

He went back to camp and had Abby get back into the trees with her Henry. She had become a good shot during the time they had been married. Ronnie eased back away from the fire a bit and waited to see if the rider was going to be a problem or not, you just couldn't be too cautious.

When the rider called the camp, Ronnie told him to come in slow and keep talking. When the rider came forward and stopped Ronnie heard a small noise off to his left a little. Ronnie asked the rider what he was doing still on the trail this late.

"Well," he said, "I was just about ready to find a spot to camp for the night when I smelled your fire."

Ronnie said, it looks like your horse is about done in, how far have you come today?

The rider said he had come from Cold Springs and was heading to Spring Creek to see a friend. As the rider talked he kept his horse side stepping a little to Ronnie's right trying to make it look like it was the horse's idea.

Ronnie said, "I think you need to be moving along. I don't think I need any company this evening thank you."

The rider asked, "how about selling me one of your extra horses, mine is about done in."

"No, they are not for sale. I am heading to California and will need them myself." About that time the rider started to reach for his pistol, but he was too late. Ronnie palmed his Colt and let her fly. He had felt he was going to try to kill him and was ready when the rider had started his move. Ronnie let two shots go and had dropped into a crouch. That is when he heard Abby's .44 bark two times on his left. Ronnie had taught her to shoot at least two times when you shoot at someone.

There must have been another man on his left that made the small noise he had heard. When Abby shot, a bullet had whipped by his head high and wide. That is when he heard a man yell "Damn you. You kilt me."

Ronnie walked over to check the man Abby had shot. She was shaking and crying and mumbling "I had to shoot him. I had to shoot him Ronnie! He just pulled up and was going to shoot you." Ronnie looked at the man Abby shot, he had a bullet hole in his left shoulder and Abby had hit him twice again just under the arm pit. Ronnie said, "I think we have found the stagecoach robbers, what do you think? Remember the Pony Express rider telling us about the Mexican hitting another one of the robbers in the shoot out? This must be the one that Juan shot."

Abby asked "what are we going to do with them?

"Well, we will take the guns and horses to the next Pony Express Station and tell them where they lay. If they want to come get them they can, they may have a reward out for them" Ronnie answered.

"We will just head on to California. I have no feelings for anyone who tried to kill me. That man you shot just missed me. If you had not shot him he would have got me. I heard a little noise on my left but I never saw him. I was lucky you were ready and killed him." When riding into the Pony Express station they were informed the two men had rewards out on them. Ronnie told the station manager the location and gave him the horses and guns to sell.

"We are riding west and hoping for no more trouble but we will be ready if need be," he told the man. The rest of the way on to Buckland Station was a nice ride, camping on water when they could and doing without when needed. Ronnie was finding out that his wife was one tough girl.

With Buckland Station in sight, they rode at a little faster pace. Because the bridge closed early they rode into the Carson River and came out behind the station.

Ronnie was putting up the horses and Abby went in to get them a room and tell them they would eat dinner. Everyone wanted to know about their trip and why they were back so soon. They had someone at their table all during dinner talking.

They had a great time and found out what was going on at the fort and around Buckland Station. With dinner finished, they walked out to the banks of the Carson River and had fun talking about when they held hands there and kissed.

Ronnie reached around and gave her breast a little squeeze and said, "we may want to go to bed a little early, if you like that idea." Taking her hand they headed back to their room. After an early breakfast they headed on to Carson City Ronnie wanted to talk to Bolivar Roberts about the telegraph lines heading to Sacramento and what that meant for the Pony Express.

The trip on in was an easy ride and no one bothered them along the way. When they got into Carson City. Ronnie found Bolivar at the station and he introduced Abby to him. Bolivar asked them to dinner. Ronnie had been right. They would shut down the Pony Express when the wires got over to Sacramento.

Bolivar asked how long would they be in town. Ronnie said they would be heading out in the morning for California.

The ride over the Sierras was just great. They could feel the heat starting when they reached the valley floor on the other side of the Sierras.

Dandy is watching the sun go down behind the hills. We are enjoying the last of the light before heading back to the barn.

Chapter 26 CALIFORNIA RANCO

Turning north, they headed out to find the large Rancho that belonged to Juanita's family. Ronnie felt they it would take a few days to find the way to the rancho. With some directions from a local trading post they rode in to the yard at the Hacienda midday two days later. Juanita came out to greet Ronnie and Abby. One of the stable men came out to take their horses.

Inside the house was cool and Ronnie asked how it stayed this cool when it was hot outside. She said it is the adobe walls. Juanita went to get her mother who was in taking care of her father. He had been bedridden from the time they found out Victor had been killed. Juanita introduced her Mother, Victoria to Abby and Ronnie. Victoria was a small woman with fine features. After the introductions she said that she would need to go back to her husband.

Juanita told Ronnie and Abby her father just heart broken about his two sons. Victoria had turned everything over to Juanita to look after she felt the rancho was lost and they would have to move.

Juanita started to tell them about what she found out when she got home. Victor had been shot and no one knew who did it, but finding out about the horse gave them some ideas about the man. They thought it was Jon Harding, or Dugan, he was called by both names. He was wanted for three killings that they knew about just in Sacramento alone.

Ronnie asked "What about your other brother, Juanita?

"He is also lost to us. He has gambled away the Rancho. We owe more than we could ever raise by selling the stock. I think we will just take my mother and father back to Nevada. He is in bad health. As it looks, he may not live out the year. The doctor thinks he has a bad heart."

Ronnie asked "have you and Juan talked about this? What do you want to do about the problem with the Rancho, I am ready to help."

Juanita answered "We would like to save the Rancho if we could, but we don't see how with so much debt and the loss of our cattle. Juan is out looking over the stock now. We still have some of the best horses in California, but they can't cover the debt either. Juan thinks my no good brother has sold off much of our cattle to cover his gambling debts."

"Juanita, do you think you could buy back the debt if you had the money?" Ronnie asked.

"Well, yes" Juanita said, "but it is a lot of money and they want cash or they will take the ranch in about thirty days."

"How much cash would it take to cover the gambling debts? "What condition is the Rancho in now? If you could get the Rancho back would it make a profit above the operating costs?" Ronnie kept asking questions.

"Juan and I have been looking at the books and we think it would do well. My father started to grow fruit trees a few years back and we have plenty of water from the river. My brother just gambled it all away."

Ronnie said, "What about your older brother?

"He is in jail in Sacramento for killing a man. There is a good chance he will be hanged in a few weeks. Juan talked to a lawyer in Sacramento last week. His name is Mr. Paul Smith. From what Mr. Smith said, there was not any way to save him. He shot a man down in front of many people and the man he shot was not armed, so it is murder."

Ronnie asked if Mr. Smith knew about the gambling house that held the ranch title, Juanita said he did. Ronnie then said "Would it be ok, if I went into town and had a talk with Mr. Smith about the title?"

Juan came in from checking on the condition of the stock and ranch's overall condition. He had been out for two days with the foreman. Juanita asked us all to come to the table so we could talk about their problem of how to save the Rancho.

Juan said that from what he had seen there were lots of cattle missing but the range was in good condition and would support about ten thousand head. The tally sheet said they had only about twenty five hundred head of cows on the range now.

He had taken time to look at the horse herd and they were still in great shape. Juan said he was thinking if they couldn't save the ranch they could gather the stock and horses and make a drive to the ranch in Nevada.

Juan said, "Ronnie, our range would hold what we have plus the twenty five hundred from here. What about making a drive to our ranch in Nevada?

Ronnie looked at him and said, "First, why don't I go and talk to the lawyer and see what we can do to save the Rancho. There should be some way to make some kind of a deal." The next morning Ronnie went to talk to the lawyer about the gambling house. When he was shown in to Mr. Smith's office he liked what he saw. This was a young man with a great presence about him, not showy, but confident.

Ronnie asked him about the owner of the gambling house. Mr. Smith answered "well, there are two owners. One is called Bob Stanton and the other is Joe Harding. I think they came to California at about the same time.

Ronnie blinked and said, "Mr. Smith, do you know the sheriff? If so could you ask if he could come over for a talk about another problem with those two men? We could meet for lunch if he would like.

Mr. Smith asked, "What do you need the sheriff for? Let's see if he can meet us for lunch and we can talk about this. I will send my runner over now.We should know in about ten minutes."

Sheriff Johnson walked in to the dining room just as they were sitting down. "Hi, Paul" the Sheriff said. Paul introduced Ronnie and after the sheriff sat down he asked, "Well son, what do we need to talk about?"

Ronnie told him about the rings stolen from his wife's mother after she was killed by Indians in eastern Utah and then selling them at the Stockton Trading Post. "When I gave my wife the rings she about had a breakdown."

"This is my other problem. I would like you to ride out with me to check brands on some stock on Mr. Harding's ranch east of town. I had the foreman from my friend's Rancho check on them yesterday and I believe they have stolen cattle from the rancho. No one from the family gave them a bill of sale for any cattle off the rancho. They also say they have the title for the ranch because the man you are about to hang lost money to Mr. Harding."

"Well Ronnie I think you have a good case, what do you say Paul?

Paul answered "As a lawyer I can't see that they have any legal hold on the Rancho."

Then Ronnie asked Sheriff Johnson if he could swear out a warrant for the arrest of both men for grave robbing, and stealing cattle. Ronnie hoped that they would find some altered brands when the cattle was inspected.

Paul said, "I will go back to the office and get the paperwork done."

"Sheriff Johnson can you meet us at the gambling house about noon tomorrow." Ronnie said, "this is my plan" and he told them what it was.

"Let's go out and check the brands on the cattle on Mr. Harding's ranch, if we find what we think we will you can arrest them for stolen cattle.

I will take a bank draft to cover the debt they say Juanita owes to our meeting. I will get them to sign off on the deed. After I get the signatures I will tell them we need to have another person come in to check the paper work. At that point you can make the arrest and take them both to jail. We have a plan and a damn good one, are we all ready to make that move. They all said ok.

Ronnie went back to the Rancho feeling better, this should be fun. Abby will feel better after this is all finished. Ronnie had no intension of telling anyone about the plan. Juan and Juanita will find out when they have the meeting to recover the deed to the Rancho.

The next morning Juan and Ronnie went to talk to the lawyer. Ronnie still had not told Juan what the plan was to recover the deed. On the way over to the card house, the lawyer told Ronnie this guy could try to pull a gun on us. He always has a shoulder holster under his left arm.

Ronnie told him that was good information to know. They walked into the card room and were escorted back to the private office of Mr. Harding and Mr. Stanton for the meeting.

Ronnie slipped off the leather thong on the hammer on his pistol and eased it in the holster, telling the lawyer and Juan to stay on his left side. The two owners were waiting for them in the back office. Mr. Harding said "Let's get to the paperwork so you can get your deed."

Ronnie asked if the deed was ready to sign and Harding said it was.

"Do you have the bank draft to cover the debt?" Mr. Harding wanted to know and Ronnie said yes. After taking a seat the lawyer pulled out the bank draft and laid it on Harding's desk.

Mr. Harding reached for the bank draft and started to jump up reaching for his gun at the same time. Now he was looking down the barrel of Ronnie's Colt. He hadn't even seen Ronnie pull his iron.

Ronnie said, "I will say this only once - remove your hand from that gun or I will kill you as you stand, do you understand? Now get me the deed and you both will sign it before you get the draft." Mr. Harding went to a safe in the wall and started to open it, Ronnie said "don't even think about pulling another gun with the paperwork."

Ronnie told Mr. Harding to ease out the pistol and lay it on the desk. Then he told Mr. Stanton to do the same. "I would not want to shoot anyone who was just trying to scratch an itch."

Mr. Harding had the deed on the desk and he signed it. "Now Mr. Stanton, you sign under his name." Ronnie said. "If I find you, or any one of your men on the Rancho, I will shoot you or them on the spot, do you also understand that?"

The gambler sat back down and was looking rather pale. Ronnie said, "we will be going now and let's not ever meet again. Oh, and just one other thing, Mr. Stanton would you get our guest from the front, he has some information you may need to know."

When Mr. Stanton opened the door he was looking at a pistol pointed at him by the Sacramento Sheriff Johnson. "Mr. Stanton would you turn around and place your hands behind you." Mr. Harding reached for his pistol but Ronnie hit him in the forehead with his pistol knocking him to the floor. Sheriff Johnson said, "Thanks, that should make it easier to get the irons on him."

When Ronnie and Juan got back to the Rancho with the deed signed free and clear Juanita started to cry. Ronnie smiled and said "well, I guess Abby and I will be going back to Nevada without you two. Juan looked at the deed and told Juanita that they needed to go down to Mr. Smith's law office and have Ronnie and Abby listed as one half owner of the Rancho. Juan said, "when you start to Sacramento we will ride with you and get the paperwork finished in the morning." The following day, after the papers were signed, Ronnie and Abby said goodbye and rode toward Sacramento to finish their honeymoon in style.

Abby asked Ronnie how rich he thought they were now that they also owned part of another ranch. He answered "well, I would say we still have four full bags of gold plus part of this Rancho. I never gave them the bank draft, the Sheriff told me to keep the draft for our trouble. Juan and his foreman will be going out to recover the stolen cattle in the morning."

Abby smiled and said "I think we can stay at a nice hotel if you want to, but who's money do we use your, or mine, or both of ours. What I want is a big brass tub full of water with both of us in it together, what do you think?"

"Ronnie said," do you think we can both fit?

Abby winked and said "You do know I am the boss, right?" Abby looked at Ronnie and asked if it was a little hard to sit in the saddle.

When they got to town they took the best room they could find and it did have a big copper tub and everything fit just like they planned. They found some shows and took a ride on the river boat San Francisco to see the sights, but after a week they were ready to start home.

On their way out of Sacramento they stopped at a bank and deposited the gold. When they got back to the Rancho they found ten golden mares ready to go. Juan was sending them back to the ranch for Teddy. Juanita had gone to see her girlfriend and purchase six chestnut mares from another Palomino breeder so as to keep the blood lines clean. At best they will still only have a 50% chance of getting a palomino foal. Juan and Ronnie talked about trading some bulls the next spring. They could meet on top of the Sierra's to make the swap. Ronnie said he would talk to Sam Applegate and see if he wanted to join them in the trade.

Abby was going to miss Juanita and the two little kids but Juanita was home and it looked like she was ready to stay. Ronnie and Abby started early the next day, leading five chestnut mares each. This would make a nice addition to the ranch. They would give Tony a part of the ranch operation when they got back, knowing that he would earn it over time.

Chapter 27 TONY FINDS TWO NEW RANCH HANDS

Tony was working the high country, moving some of the cattle to a new valley when out of the trees came two Indians riding slow in his direction. He pulled his Henry and reined up to see what was going on with the two Indians. They just kept coming and kept their rifles across their legs. When they got close Tony could see one of them was the Indian they had saved. When they got close, they raised their right arms and smiled at him. The one he recognized pointed to the cattle and moved his hand like they would help him move the cows also.

Tony slid the rifle back into the scabbard and started pushing the cattle along. The Indians moved off to each side and for sure they were going to help. When they got the cattle settled into a new little valley Tony started to look for some water and a place to make camp. Turning back the way they had just come, he pointed to a small draw with willows coming out on to the flats that meant there was water and good grass.

Tony stepped down and started setting up camp. One of the Indians started to gather wood to get a fire going. Tony still could not figure this out; did he now have two Indians as ranch hands, or what?

Using sign language Tony started to figure out they did want to work around the ranch to learn about cattle. Tony started to show them different things and saying the words. The Indians were trying to say them also. This went on for a few days. The three of them moved cattle and cleaned out some water holes. The work in the high country was done - now what would they do?

When he started to pack up his kit, they did the same and when he started back to the ranch they came along with him. Getting back to the ranch he showed them a place in the barn to stay. When Tony got up the next morning, the two Indians were working with the fillies and the colt.

When he had some food ready they came over and ate on the porch and then went back working with the horses. Tony knew he would need some meat soon so he went out and drew a picture of a deer in the dirt, saying the word "deer".

Then he lifted his arm like he was going to shoot. They understood what he was saying. They got their horses and rode off to the north. Later that day they came back with an elk, each was packing half of it. The Indians were beginning to understand some words. They told Tony the one he had saved was called White Bird and the other was called Tee who was White Bird's younger brother. White Bird said "deer small, elk big much good." He was right, elk meat was much better and all this would last for some time. White Bird cut off a leg and went out to hang it in the barn.

Tony needed to go to Mr. Brown's store for supplies, but how would he tell White Bird and Tee he was going, and would be back in a few days? Using a stick he started to draw in the dirt. He did his best to let them know what he was going to do.

The next thing is, how do I tell them to just keep working with the young horses? After he loaded the wagon and started out he looked back and they were at the corral working with the stud colt.

Tony stopped by Sam and Beth's place and asked if they wanted him to pickup any thing for them. Little John asked if he could ride in-he needed some stuff. Sam said they were ok and he would be going in a week or so anyway. Tony and Little John started out. This would make for a better trip. Little John started asking about the Indians Tony was working with. He said Mom and Pop said you should watch your hair, they like the curly hair like yours. Your top knot would make a good scalp to hang on their horse's bridle.

They talked about Tony trying to talk to them, and that they were getting some of the words, but mostly he just drew pictures on the ground and pointed a lot, but they were getting along just fine. Little John thought it was funny when Tony told him about White Bird bringing their mares to be bred by Diamond. Tony said, "we figured it better than having him stealing Diamond." Tony was telling Little John what do you think they want to work on a ranch for anyway? I guess when we start to talk I will find out some day. Mr. Browns store was getting bigger each time they came to town.

When riding in Tony saw a wagon down by the stream and it looked like some one was living there. Tony asked Mr. Brown what was going on with the wagon. He said they were heading west but one of their horses died when they got here, so they had to stop here for a while to try and get another horse to pull the wagon.

You will meet Maggie in a minute She is helping me around the store, and her father, Sean O'Reilly is driving the team doing deliveries, using the wagon Ronnie is letting me use while he is gone. Mrs. O'Reilly died on the way out, just got sick and died. Maggie came out of the back room with some cloth and came up short when she got a look at Tony. Mr. Brown said, "Maggie this is Tony." They both said hi.

"Tony working on a ranch a few days ride north. The wagon and team your dad is driving belongs to the ranch. Maggie, why don't you get some coffee and you two sit down at the table over there and get acquainted."

"Tony will tell you what he will need. You can have a break. You have been working all day. Tony would you like some food? It is about dinner time." "Why not," he said. "It was nice to talk to a girl for a change." Little John came in and joined them. He met Maggie also.

Maggie got up and gave Mr. Brown the list and they set about to fill it. Tony kept looking at Maggie and she caught him a few times and smiled. Tony caught her looking a couple of times also. When Maggie came back he said, "I have never seen hair as red as yours."

He added quickly that it sure looks nice. Maggie smiled and said thanks. Mr. Brown said you guys are going to spend the night, right? Tony said they were and would head back in the morning some time.

Tony added the view is getting better around here, "I may stay over another night if you don't mind." Mr. Brown said Maggie may just like that herself, I think she would like someone her own age to talk to, she is a real nice girl.

You may want to sit on the porch after I close and you could tell her all about this part of the country. Tony asked Maggie if she would like to sit out after she got off work for a while. She said, "sure I would like that." The sun was setting in the west, the sky was awash in red when they sat down to talk. Tony told her about the ranch he was working on and having the two Indians helping him. They both said that was different but time will tell what they want.

She got him to talk about the other ranch he had worked on further east from here. He started telling about how they handle the cattle and about his love of training horses. When he told her about how he got the Palomino stud she put her hand over her mouth, and said, "oh my god you could have been killed."

They talked some more about horses on the ranch. She then told him that she rode jumpers in Scotland before coming to America. Tony asked her to tell him about her life in Scotland. Maggie said, "it is getting late and my father will come looking for me soon." Tony said he would walk her back to the wagon, she said ok. On the way to the wagon their hands touched, then intertwined and stayed that way, each taking a peek to see if it was ok.

With a little squeeze, they walked on to the wagon. Maggie called to her dad when they got close to the wagon. Sean came to the fire and Maggie told him this is Tony, he is working on a ranch north of here a day or two. They are raising cattle and horses and Tony has a Palomino stallion. He got it when a man tried to kill him and Ronnie Campbell when they were delivering horses to the Pony Express at Spring Creak Station. They talked about horses for a while and then Tony said he needed to head back to feed the stock.

Maggie walked out around the wagon holding his hand and said good night. "Will I see you in the morning?" Tony said, "I am staying another day so we can talk some more. I like you and want you to tell me about your trip over to America.

In the morning when Tony and Little John went in to eat, Maggie was delivering food to a table with an older couple, Tony had seen the wagon parked in front of the store when he came in to eat. Maggie said to sit down and I will bring you some coffee. We thought you worked in the store. She said, "I do what is needed." Tony said just get me a steak and eggs if you have them. Little John said that is good for me.

Tony was hanging around the store trying to talk to Maggie when Mr. Brown turned to Tony and asked him if he would take Maggie out to a small ranch with some supplies for Mrs. Wilson. Mrs. Wilson has some stuff she would not want a man delivering to her. With the wagon loaded they started off to the south on a small wagon trail leading to her ranch. Maggie slid over on the wagon seat close to Tony. He looked over and smiled and met her eyes they was smiling to. Reaching the ranch, Tony pulled the wagon up to the back of the house.

Maggie had just jumped down when Mrs. Wilson came out of the back door of her house. "Maggie, we can just unload the boxes into the back room," She told Tony they could take care of the unloading. So he could just stay on the wagon seat and wait for them to finish.

When they started back to the store Tony said, "what did she not want me to see?" Well, she is a dress maker and also makes women's undergarments. Her work room is the back room we unloaded the supplies into. She sells her under garments to the wagon trains when they come through heading west. Mrs. Wilson thinks men should never see what we wear, don't you think that is funny? Mom used to hang her stuff inside of her dresses, when she did the wash.

Tony pulled the team to a stop and turned to Maggie and asked if he could kiss her. Maggie said, "what took you so long? I would have let you kiss me last night but you just walked off. Why do you think I walked you around behind the wagon last night? You just went back to the barn to go to sleep."

"Well to my defense, I did think about you most of the night." Tony turned and kissed her real good this time. During the ride back to the store they talked about her life in Scotland and the trip across the country to Nevada. When they got back, Mr. Brown asked if he got to unload and smiled. "Thanks Tony, for helping I thought you two may want to talk being you are about the same age and all."

"Did you keep Little John busy while we made the delivery?" "Some" he said Sean and Little John worked on the wagons a bit. They had time to grease the wheels on two of the wagons, one of Ronnie's was about dry so it was a good thing we got it done.

"So you will be heading back in the morning?" "Yes he said, "I need to get back to check on the cattle and horses." Little John said that you had two Indians working on the ranch. Well I am not sure if they are working or they just showed up and started doing stuff. I am waiting for Ronnie to get back to see what to do about them. I sure don't want to make them mad at me, I like my hair as it is.

Tony sat out again with Maggie on the porch and got in a whole lot of kissing, Tony had been asking a lot of questions and it was clear they really liked each other. When it was getting late he just came out with it and said. Look, Maggie, I live a three day ride back in the hills, I will not be able to come back for a month or so. Would you like to marry me when I come back to town next trip into town?

Do I need to talk to your father about us? Damn I don't know if you want to marry me. Maggie said, "yes, I would like to marry you, and yes you do need to talk to my dad." Well lets go and get this out of the way. They walked down to the wagon still holding hands and talking low.

Sean was setting by the fire with a cup of coffee. He got up when they came around the wagon. "Well, you again," "Yes, it is me; I would like to ask you if I could marry your daughter." "Well, have you asked her or are you asking me?" "No I mean yes, I have asked her." "Well what did she say?" "She said yes." "Well, Tony I guess that is a yes from both of us." "Could we get married when I come back to town next month?"

After talking to Sean Maggie lead Tony down by the stream. Laying down a blanket she picked up at the wagon they lay down holding each other and started to kiss. The night was dark with the sky full of stars they, explored each other.

Tony had unbuttoned her top and was touching her breast then he leaned over and placed his mouth over her nipple and pulled her nipple with his lips. Maggie started to take her dress off when Tony said "no lets wait until we get married." Maggie had reached and found him hard and she could feel him pulsing through his pants. "Do we have to wait Maggie asked? "I want you now she said. We better get back or it will be too late. "What I think we need to do is find a preacher and do this right."

In the morning, with the wagon loaded, Tony got a send off kiss that would help make the month go fast. Little John was driving when they headed back north to the ranch. Little John poked Tony in the ribs and said, "well, that didn't take long." Tony said, "we sure hit it off right away. This is going to be the longest month I have ever had to live. I don't even know where we are going to live, but we will work it out."

"Well Tony you had better get building a house and make it fast." "What am I going to do? Ronnie and Abby don't even know I have two Indians working on the ranch and now I asked Maggie to marry me and I don't own anything but a Palomino stallion and a couple of guns. That is not much to get started with."

Ronnie and Abby got back to Mr. Brown's store a few days after Tony had headed back with supplies. Mr. Brown asked Ronnie if he knows a preacher. "Why do you ask about a preacher?" "You need to meet a new member of your family." What are you talking about?" Well, come over and meet Maggie, Tony has asked Maggie to get married next month when he comes back to get more supplies."

Ronnie and Abby asked Maggie to come over and sit down and eat with them, and tell them about Tony. She just lit up when she told them about meeting him and falling in love. They just looked at each other thinking does that sound just like us.

Maggie asked them to come and meet her dad. He had just came back in from delivering a load of supplies to an outlying ranch. Maggie called her dad over and told him this is the owners of the ranch Tony is working on.

Abby jumped in and said. "What do you mean working on?" He and his brother are part owners of two ranches - one here and the other in California. Maggie said Tony thinks he is just a ranch hand. Well we will take care of that just as soon as we get back to the ranch, Maggie.

Ronnie asked Mr. O'Reilly what other kind of work he can do besides driving a team and making deliveries out to Mr. Brown's customers. "Well I have been in mining all of my life." Ronnie and Abby looked at each other and smiled.

Ronnie said, "look Maggie how about you and your dad come on up to the ranch for a while? You and Tony can get to know each other better and we can get a preacher headed this way."

"Mr. O'Reilly you say you know about mining: How would you like to help me get a gold mine in operation?" "When do we leave? he asked. I do have a problem, I only have one horse." "My other one died after we got here and I have been stuck." "Well, let's do this. In the morning we will hitch the team you have been driving to your wagon and we will all go home to the ranch."

"I will send some help back with a fresh team and pick up my wagon with the supplies I am ordering now." With the sun coming up, they all headed north on the wagon road leading to their new home. Maggie asked if she could ride one of the horses during the trip to the ranch. Ronnie pulled out one of the new saddles he had ordered from Mr. Brown and saddled one of the new chestnut mares for her to ride.

Maggie felt alive being in the saddle again. She told Abby this western saddle is different from her English one when she used to ride jumpers in Scotland. Ronnie and Abby could tell this girl had been riding for many years, she would be additional help on the ranch working cattle.

When they reached the ranch Ronnie could see three riders heading toward the ranch house. He could see the big blond stud but what were the other two riding with him? It was not long when they reached the ranch yard and pulled up. Tony was off his horse and ran to Maggie asking. "What are you doing here? This is good right?"

Then everyone was talking except White Bird and Tee. They just picked up the reins and led the horses to the corrals and started stripping the tack and feeding. Ronnie just stood and watched. No one even told them what to do. When Tony turned around Ronnie asked him, "what's this, when did we get Indians working on the ranch."

Tony said, "do you remember White Bird? He is the one Juan and I fixed his leg and arm. Well, he just came back a few weeks ago and started helping me move cattle in the high country. When I started back to the ranch they came along. When I got up the next day they were working with the yearlings.

They have that young stud doing things I have never seen done with horses that young. Tony asked Ronnie what was Mr. O'Reilly doing with him. "Well lets put it this way, we are going to open a gold mine. Mr. O'Reilly knows how to set up a mine."

Ronnie said, "Tony, look at me," and Abby said "look at me at the same time." "Now get Maggie and listen to this. You are not just a ranch hand, you are like your brother, you are a part owner of this ranch, and on top of that you are part owner of the ranch in California and all of us standing in this yard will all be owners of the gold mine when Mr. O'Reilly gets it going." "Now partners who do you think we can find to fix dinner? I am ready to eat." Tony and Maggie had drifted off and were walking down by the river. "I don't think they are hungry". Abby said!

The end,

I hope you enjoyed reading this book as much as I did writing it. Ruby Gold I hope will allow all of the players to fulfill their potential, both in life and in what you as a reader though they should or could become in your imagination.

Ronnie Campbell Series
Ruby Gold Book 2

Tony was pulling out of a wash and the front wheel hit a rock with a jerk, he fell forward in the seat. That's when he felt the whip of a bullet pass by his head. He then heard the rifle report. Ducking down in the seat he slapped the reins down on the horse's rumps and they were off at a hard run. Looking back, Tony could see two men riding hard to catch the wagon, from time to time they would shoot at him.

The campsite was just ahead now. He knew when he reached it he would have some cover behind the trees. Reaching the trees Tony pulled the team to a stop, jumped off the wagon and pulling out his Henry and returned fire. He fired six quick shots and stopped. Whoever was shooting at him might think he had an older Spencer rifle. It worked. As he was feeding shells into the rifle he saw the men mount and start toward him running hard, thinking his rifle was empty.

His Henry was reloaded now with all fifteen rounds. Moving to a new position he was ready to fire when he heard shots coming from behind the men. Looking up he saw Abby and Maggie firing at the men with their horses at a dead run.

Abby and Maggie had heard the shooting from about a mile out from the campsite. Pulling their rifles, levering a shell into the chamber they were ready. Both girls were leaning forward in the saddle, taking the reins in their left hand, using their legs to smooth out the ride to help with aiming the rifles. They came in at a full gallop, both rifles were talking. With bullets coming from two directions, now Joe and Bob rode for cover in a small draw.

Tony also started to fire at the men who were now in a cross fire. The two men turned back into the trees covering the hills, but not before one was hit by the girls' fire. Maggie pulled her horse to a sliding stop and jumped off to see if Tony was ok. Abby asked Tony, "what was that about?" Tony said, "I was just pulling out of the wash back down the road a bit when a bullet went past my head. If it had not been for that rock bouncing the wagon I would have been killed. I keep telling myself I am going to get a team down here and pull that rock out of the way. I am never going to move it now. That is what saved my life."

Abby said, "we need to get Ronnie and start tracking these two. I wonder who they are?" Maggie was talking to Tony about what could have caused someone to shoot at him. Tony used Maggie's horse to ride back to the last place the men had been seen. When he got to the little draw they had rode into Tony found some blood on the ground. "So, one of them is wounded." Walking along their tracks he could tell that the horses were large with a long stride, they could be Thoroughbreds and one had a special bar shoe on the right rear.

Riding back to the campsite Tony found a fire going and some dinner being cooked. The girls asked if he thought they should push on all night to get back to the ranch earlier so they could warn Ronnie about the shooting. "No, let's just keep watch tonight and hit the trail early. Why don't you cook some extra so we can just get up and start early?"

Everyone was up early. The sun was still behind the hills, just beginning to show some light. The wagon was loaded and horses saddled. They started back to the ranch. They would stop at the Applegate ranch to inform them to keep an eye out for the two men. They all knew that Ronnie was going to ride over to see Sam about the hauling of equipment but figured he would be back to the ranch by the time they get there.

ABOUT RON BELL

Ron Bell has just turned the big 70 and this is his first book. The second book is started and should be ready in about November of this year.

Ron is active in the Pony Express and is still active in the Chamber of Commerce and many other projects in and around Silver Springs Nevada.

Made in the USA
San Bernardino, CA
09 May 2013